PART 1

FOX ON THE RUN

The West Side Kid

The West Side Kid

a novel

Valentine Cardinale

iUniverse, Inc.
New York   Bloomington

Copyright © 2009 by Valentine Cardinale

All rights reserved. No part of this book may be used or reproduced by any means, graphic, electronic, or mechanical, including photocopying, recording, taping or by any information storage retrieval system without the written permission of the publisher except in the case of brief quotations embodied in critical articles and reviews.

This is a work of fiction. All of the characters, names, incidents, organizations, and dialogue in this novel are either the products of the author's imagination or are used fictitiously.

iUniverse books may be ordered through booksellers or by contacting:

iUniverse
1663 Liberty Drive
Bloomington, IN 47403
www.iuniverse.com
1-800-Authors (1-800-288-4677)

Because of the dynamic nature of the Internet, any Web addresses or links contained in this book may have changed since publication and may no longer be valid. The views expressed in this work are solely those of the author and do not necessarily reflect the views of the publisher, and the publisher hereby disclaims any responsibility for them.

ISBN: 978-1-4401-4390-8 (sc)
ISBN: 978-1-4401-4392-2 (dj)
ISBN: 978-1-4401-4391-5 (ebook)

Printed in the United States of America

iUniverse rev. date: 05/15/2009

Dedicated to the memory of

MARY PATRICIA

The prettiest girl on the West Side

1

It was almost dusk. Lorne Bennett, who was calling himself Peter Fox these days, strolled out of the convenience store and into the parking lot. For a change, he felt like a normal person, part of the human race, rather than a fugitive from justice. He brushed away any thought that he was the celebrated movie actor accused of murdering his wife and then abandoning his baby daughter twenty-two years earlier.

Halfway to his car, he stopped and gazed up in awe at the splashes of fuchsia and gold in the western sky. He took off his cowboy hat, scratched his head. Wasn't this the same sky he saw growing up on New York City's West Side? Why, then, was it so much more spectacular here in the Arizona desert? He didn't need answers. It was enough just to watch the unfolding beauty of a sunset, one of the few pleasures he had left in his life.

He also enjoyed reminiscing about the old days. With a smile he tried to hide, he often thought about those carefree times growing up on the streets of New York and that hectic, exciting period when his career took off in Hollywood. When he could bear it, he also harked back to some of the happier, more intimate moments he shared with his wife before the baby came along and their relationship soured. Now, more than two decades later, he still couldn't believe Aurora was gone. Shot to death at age thirty-one in their elegant Manhattan apartment, while their four-month-old daughter Laura slept nearby. And here he was, still under suspicion for that crime, still on the run.

A container of hot tea in one hand and the *Arizona Republic* tucked under his arm, Lorne headed for his dull green Camry, which sat lonely and unnoticed in a corner of the parking lot. On a busy roadway nearby, a bearded man in a frayed red T-shirt and denim shorts sputtered by in his Suzuki, waving to anyone in sight as he passed. Lorne gave a half-wave, though he was almost sure he didn't know the man. There was something about the friendly openness of the biker that made him smile, and he felt more than a little envious.

After climbing into the car, he turned on the AC full blast. It had been another scorcher, "a cool 110 degrees," said one TV meteorologist Lorne felt had been in the August sun too long. Lorne had been living in the Arizona desert for almost five years now, and, yes, it was less humid compared with points East, but hot was hot. Moreover, short- and long-range predictions for the area were for even hotter, drier weather, which didn't seem to stem the flow of transplants and "snow birds" into the Valley. To them, this was paradise. To Lorne, who was fitting in nicely with the western lifestyle, it almost felt like home.

In no hurry, he removed the lid from the container and took a couple of sips of tea, remembering something his mother used to tell him when he was a boy. "Nothing like a nice, hot cup of tea on a hot summer day." How often had he heard her say that? As a boy, Lorne brushed aside her words, interpreting them merely as an Irish mother's fondness for tea, which was near the bottom of his beverage preferences. "But, mama, do you think they drink hot tea in Africa?" he'd challenge her. "If they can get it, of course," she'd reply.

Long after his mother's death, he gave a broader interpretation to her simple secret for coping with the heat. Sometimes it's wiser to do the opposite of what people expect you to do. He often used that strategy to break through time-worn barriers set up by overcautious studio heads, crowd-pleasing producers, and egocentric directors in his climb up the Hollywood ladder. Over the years, he also learned to tolerate tea.

Taking another sip, he noticed a boy of about three or four walking toward the edge of the parking lot, the onrushing traffic on McKelips Avenue only a dash away. Nearby, a large, frizzy-haired young woman with baggy white shorts, probably his mother, was struggling to place an infant in a car seat. She had her back to the boy who was staring out into the roadway.

If the risk were not so great, Lorne might have let the scene unfold on its own, confident the woman would discover that her toddler son was not within sight and rush to his side. But not now. "Ah, hell!" he muttered as he shut off the engine, placed his tea in the holder, and bolted out of the car.

"Whoa, whoa, where're you going, big guy?" he said, clutching the wanderer by the hand. The boy turned, looked up at the tall, wiry man with the grayish blue eyes, and let out a primeval scream as he tried to wriggle out of Lorne's grasp. The frizzy-haired woman had finally managed to secure the infant into the car seat, and when she heard her son's hysterical scream, she ran to him and yanked him away from Lorne.

"It's okay, it's okay, Mikey," she reassured her son. Then, glaring at the stranger she had already concluded was depraved, she said, "You ought to be ashamed of yourself, a man your age."

Lorne tried to explain. "He was all by himself, ma'am, and it looked like he might ..."

She almost yanked the boy's arm out of its socket as she led him back to the car. "Come on, Mikey."

Lorne tried to finish his explanation anyway, just for the record. "He might have run out into the street ... Ah, forget it!" He shrugged and started back to his car.

Suddenly, the woman stopped. Helped by the light from a nearby street lamp that had just gone on, she stared at the stranger. He was lean but well-built, probably in his late fifties, straight and tall. There was a look of hurt and weariness in his eyes along with some annoyance. Traces of tension were visible behind protruding cheekbones in his handsome, angular face.

"Don't I know you?" asked the woman.

"I doubt it, ma'am," he replied. Then, reaching his car, he added, "You might want to keep an eye on your kid. Mikey just might fool you one day."

"Oh, Mikey wouldn't do nothin.' He's afraid of his own shadow." Mikey, still sobbing, was sucking air through his nose, machine-gun style.

"You never know, lady."

"I'm sure I know you," she blurted out. "Aren't you that actor?"

Lorne was shaking his head as he drove out of the lot. Suddenly, he didn't feel normal anymore. He opened the window and poured the remnants of his tea onto the roadway. Against his mother's advice, he decided he needed a cool drink.

2

THE GLOW OF THE COMPUTER BATHED BILLY
Volpe's face in a soft blue light. A handsome man, he appeared tired
tonight. Dark circles under his eyes, coupled with a short beard and
moustache that needed trimming, made him look older than his
thirty-two years. A sigh suggested he was not completely satisfied
with what he had just written.

A reporter and photographer, he took pride in his work. As a
stringer for several local newspapers in the Valley, he covered a
broad range of topics, from family disputes, break-ins, accidents,
and brush fires to visits to the area by dignitaries, celebrities, and
other assorted characters. The work was interesting, feeding his
boundless curiosity, and gave him a pleasant lifestyle, but it was
not likely to make him rich.

To compensate for any financial shortcomings, Billy told
himself that being his own boss meant he could work at his own
pace, at home, and close to his family, which these days consisted
of a twelve-year-old daughter, Alexandra—or Alex, as she liked
to be called. While the constant deadlines sometimes cut into his
personal time, they didn't bother him. Instead, his ability to meet
deadlines earned him a splendid reputation for dependability
among the local media.

If there was a sore spot at all, it was the nagging feeling that this could be all there was when it came to his career. Any dream he had in his youth of being the editor of a major daily had long ago faded.

"Do you know what I need now?" he'd often tell his daughter.

"What?" she'd ask.

"The big story," he'd reply. "You know, the one everyone wants, but only you get. Do you know what that would mean?"

She'd nod. He'd told her before.

He'd tell her again anyway. "Bigger and better assignments. And that would mean more prestige and respect, which would mean more opportunities and, of course, the big bucks."

"Don't worry, dad. You'll find the big one someday," she assured him. And he'd hug her for her confidence in him.

As Billy searched for the perfect finish to the article he was writing tonight—about the Tempe man who claimed to have found a nugget of gold in his dog's stool—he sensed that this was not the big story he was searching for, but, hey, you never know. He finally clicked off the computer and rose from his cluttered desk. He hesitated for a moment, as if he were going to sit down again, but then walked into the kitchen where he found Alex.

"Finished?" she asked, never lifting her eyes from the Nancy Drew mystery she was reading.

"Think so."

"Me, too," she said, closing the book.

"I'll give it one more edit before sending it off," said Billy.

She poured him the cup of coffee she knew he'd ask for and placed it in front of him. In the background, a TV newscaster droned on about the outlook for gay marriages in several states.

"Are you gay, dad?" she inquired, always ready for a good controversy.

"Don't think so," he replied, a smile slipping across his face.

Apparently, he wasn't biting. "Can I read your story, dad?"

Billy hesitated for a moment. "Okay. Only don't change anything. I'm on deadline."

The phone rang. Alex turned to her father. "Another assignment," she predicted.

Billy picked up the remote and turned down the TV.

Alex snapped up the phone. "Oh hi, Trudi." Billy raised his eyebrows. He knew that Trudi, Alex's mother who lived in Seattle, frequently called to see how the girl was doing.

"Yes, I know it's been a while," said Alex. "What, almost a week?" Billy watched with interest as Alex fielded a barrage of questions. He thought about the woman on the other end of the phone ...

Billy had known Trudi Dineen ever since his family moved to Arizona from Michigan when he was eleven years old. By their late teens, Billy and Trudi were madly in love and decided to get married. But after a short engagement, they scrapped their wedding plans and rented an apartment in Mesa. Soon after, Trudi gave birth to a beautiful girl with dark eyes and light brown hair as fine as corn silk. They named her Alexandra.

For the first few months, Billy proudly watched Trudi do everything a model mom should do. Then, one evening, the bubble burst. "I'm going out," Trudi announced. "I need a night out with the girls. I'll be back in a couple of hours. Give the baby a bottle at nine-thirty." Billy didn't say anything that night. He knew that Trudi had been feeling pretty depressed lately. Only the other night, she had told him that "the good times" were passing her by.

Two week later, Trudi went back to work and started going out with her friends again on a regular basis. At one outing, she called to say that she was not coming home that night. Over the next few weeks, Billy learned that Trudi had met someone, the handsome, fun-loving Louie Zampone who just happened to work at the same company where she worked. One evening, she made another announcement—"I'm leaving"—and ran off with Louie to Seattle.

At first, Billy was furious. He was a volcano read to erupt, but his responsible nature soon told him he had no time to explode. First, he needed someone to help him take care of the baby, especially when he was working. *Thank God for grandparents!*

Gradually, Billy came to accept his single parenthood role, even enjoy it, as he saw the kind of person his daughter was becoming. The girl blossomed into an exceptional twelve-year-old who seemed much older than her years. She was an excellent student, smart but not smug, the admiration of teachers and the envy of classmates. "Borderline gifted" was the way one school administrator described her. Her father also knew her as a sweet, loving girl, somewhat of a worrier who sometimes wore him out with questions on a broad range of subjects. She gobbled up mystery stories, which she tried to solve for herself even before the author revealed an ending she didn't always accept ...

Billy took another sip of coffee as Alex finished talking with her mother on the phone. It was his turn now. "Hi, Trudi. Yeah, she's doing fine ... right ... right. You don't say? How much do you need? Sure ... sure. Say hello to Louie." He hung up, slightly dazed.

"Well, how much does she need?" asked Alex.

"A couple of hundred. She's in a credit card bind."

Alex rolled her eyes. "Aren't we all?"

3

As Lorne Bennett joined the traffic winding West, he felt uneasy. *Did the frizzy-haired woman really know who I was, and did she write down my license plate number?* It had been months since someone had claimed to recognize him. The last time, an elderly woman in a supermarket began shaking her cane at him. "I know you! You're what's-his-name." Fortunately, she could not remember what's-his-name, but since then Lorne had become more wary.

Even with his gift for changing his appearance through an array of disguises, he continued to worry that someone would spot him. Passers-by occasionally gave him more than a casual glance, and if one of his movies came on to the TV in a bar, he'd pay for his drink and retreat.

The traffic flowed North now toward a popular gambling casino, and Lorne went with it. It was a trick he had learned a long time ago as a celebrity living in a big city. Sometimes the best way to escape the crowds is to go where the crowds are—a busy street or a large shopping mall, where no one wants to know your name or gives you a second look. Judging by the number of vehicles in the parking lot, this looked like a perfect place to stop.

He opened the door of the casino and walked into a cacophony of pings and flashing things. And it was only Monday. Apparently, humanity's quest for jackpots knows no day off. All around, men with shadowy faces and pale-faced women in wrinkled shorts—some working several machines at a time—pressed buttons and pulled levers with desperate determination. One slots player celebrated the ding, ding, ding, ding of a winning machine with whoops of pure joy. This was an ideal place for a quick drink.

Lorne carved his way through the smoke to the bar. "I'll have a tall Pepsi with lots of ice and the coldest Heineken you got," he said to the pretty, blue-eyed woman behind the long bar.

"You want them together?" she asked.

"You bet," he replied, pulling up a stool.

When she returned with the drinks, she put them on the counter and smiled. "Someone's thirsty."

Lorne took a long swallow from his Pepsi as she watched. "Ah, that's great! Can I buy you a drink?"

The invitation seemed to surprise her. Apparently, such offers were rare in the casino. "Oh, no thanks. New around here?"

Lorne took a sip of beer. "Not really. How about you?"

"I'm what you call a native, born and spoiled in Apache Junction. Going to pharmacy school now. I'm in my junior year."

A smile crept across his face. "That's wonderful. Your parents must be very proud."

"They're ecstatic. They're both pharmacists. What about you? Any children?"

Lorne swung his stool nervously from side to side, not sure how to answer that. "Yes, a daughter," he finally replied. "She's about your age, maybe a couple of years older."

"What's she do?"

"She's in advertising in New York City."

"Oh, Mad Avenue?"

"Well, near there. She's a copywriter."

"Now who's proud?"

Lorne nodded, smiled, and took a gulp of beer.

The young woman began wiping the counter with a towel. "I know I'm not supposed to ask," she began.

Lorne felt his whole body tighten into a knot.

"But how're you doing out there?" She gestured toward the gaming tables and slot machines.

"Oh, excellent," he laughed. "I'm not playing."

"Between you and me, good choice. It's nice to see a winner once in a while."

"You gotta know when to fold 'em ... and when not to play 'em."

She smiled, and he couldn't help smiling back. Then, with a final swipe of her towel, she added, "Nice talking to you. Stay cool, and continued good luck."

"You, too—and good luck in pharmacy school."

She reached out to shake his hand. "My name's Amy, Amy Duncan."

Her hand was warm and soft, and she held his hand in hers longer than he expected.

"Peter Fox," he returned, as he reluctantly withdrew his hand.

"Would you like another?" she asked.

He smiled, shook his head. As he watched her walk away, he finished his drinks, then got up and left.

Lorne thought about Amy Duncan on the way home. She was lovely, friendly, caring. She'll make a nice catch for someone. He didn't know why he'd said as much as he did, or even talked with her.

Perhaps it was because she reminded him of Laura. As if he knew what his daughter was really like! All he ever saw were photos from his West Side buddies, often taken from bad angles, and once or twice a year a trusted friend would call him and bring him up to date on how or what she was doing.

Twice, Lorne drifted to the center lane, and he was beeped, barked, and fingered back into the right lane by anxious drivers probably going nowhere. Lorne had been doing a lot of that lately, drifting in mind and spirit. Usually he was drifting back to another place, another time. Tonight he drifted back to the daughter he hardly knew.

He remembered the day she was born as clearly as if it were yesterday ...

Lorne was at a meeting with his agent in Los Angeles when he received the call. Aurora had just given birth to a girl in New York, almost three weeks ahead of schedule. He could still feel the excitement and fear in the pit of his stomach when he got the news. Tom Danzig, his agent, threw his arms around Lorne in jubilation. Lorne backed away, a serious, sick look suddenly crossing his face.

"What's the matter?" asked Tom.

"I don't know," said Lorne, gazing out the window. "It scares the hell out of me."

"Oh, that's normal," said Tom. "You'll be fine."

Lorne shook his head. "Having children was not my idea. I'm not ready, Tom."

"But you had to know, Lorne. Didn't you guys talk?"

"Yes, of course," Lorne replied. "We talked and we talked, and we fought. I couldn't change her mind, and she got pregnant."

"And now the baby is here."

"Call me naive or stupid. Maybe I've been working too hard. I never thought this day would come."

"Do yourself a favor. Go to New York, Lorne. Go to New York and see your wife and your daughter."

And Lorne did. When he arrived, he put on the happiest face he could. When he saw his daughter for the first time, he was struck by her beauty, diminutive size, and vulnerability. He acted like a proud father, and part of him was, but he was frightened, too, and he wanted to run as far away as possible.

Now, as he headed home from the Arizona casino, there was another feeling churning inside him, something drawing him closer to the daughter he never knew. *Does she ever wonder about me? Will she ever forgive me for what I did? What would she say if I suddenly came into her life?*

4

Once again, Laura Bennett was slightly out of breath when she arrived at her desk in midtown Manhattan. Only four months on the job, she was determined to be the best copywriter she could be. But in a highly competitive field like advertising, she had only a small window of opportunity to prove herself. More immediately, she had to do something about this rushing around in the mornings. It was causing too much bedlam, and she had not even begun her workday!

Aware that her ad agency's meetings usually started on time, she reached into her purse and pulled out a mirror for one quick, last look. She shook her head, apparently not satisfied by what she saw. Actually, Laura was quite beautiful. She had her mother's dazzling hazel eyes and long, sun-kissed brown hair along with her father's strong, finely etched features, and she was long and lean. At twenty-two, she was still trying to complete the process of peeling off the awkward years, but she was changing and gaining confidence every day. Although she felt more comfortable in an old pair of jeans, she realized that the clothes she wore were important for the job she loved.

Today, she was wearing a tan pants suit that clung gently to her body as she entered the conference room. She was late, and all of the large, comfortable chairs were already taken. She found a no-frills, oak chair in the back of the room and wedged it, with apologies, between an account executive and a research manager. Placing a pad on the table, she sat down, took a deep breath, and looked around the table. Everyone was there. That's one of the things she really liked about the job—working closely with others as part of a team. Most of all, she enjoyed the creative process, especially the writing part—finding the right words that succinctly and quickly grabbed the customer's attention and held it for as long as it took to get the message across.

Across the table, Anita Tedesco, her friend, smiled and winked when she caught Laura's eye. Laura smiled back. Anita always helped to keep things in perspective for her. "You never know in this crazy, damn business," she told Laura one day in her well-entrenched Queens accent. A media planner known for a tough negotiating style that earned her some excellent media buys, she seldom minced words, which could be a bit salty on occasion. "We lose one or two big accounts, and, quick as a fart, you're out on your ass. 'Goodbye, Harriet! Have a nice life! Now let's all go down to Connolly's for a farewell blast!' "

Laura roared. "Oh, come on, Anita. It can't be that bad!"

"Yeah? You just watch, Ms. Everything's-Coming-Up-Roses."

As much as she was brought to tears by Anita's warnings, she couldn't dismiss them. Just to bolster her own office image, Laura regularly visited hair salons, took advantage of makeup specials at Bloomingdale's, and began building a wardrobe for work. Deep down, she felt lucky, blessed, that she had landed a nice job with a small but growing ad agency during an extremely difficult economic period.

As her Aunt Sally, who attended Mass daily, told her when she got the job, "Who says prayers aren't answered?" Uncle Roger, whom Laura sometimes called "Mr. Softie", had a more personal, emotional reaction. "I'm so proud of you," he said, fighting back tears. "You deserve nothing but the best." Their good wishes meant a lot. Sally and Roger Kent were the parents she never knew.

At work, Laura was assigned two companies—a women's shoe company and a teen cosmetics firm—and she was a member of a new business team working on a few promising accounts. One of them, a regional airline, was the subject of today's meeting.

Sumner Grady, the creative director who was leading the meeting, identified Regis Airline's problem—"It's simple. They've cut their prices to the bone, they have all types of promotional deals out there, but no one's flying their planes. I'm sure the economy has something to do with it. But, whatever the problem, it's our job to find a solution." Then, turning to the newest arrival, he said, "What do you think, Laura?"

She glanced at her notes, cleared her throat. Then, slowly but confidently, she began, "I've been thinking. Maybe it's time Regis try something new. Emphasizing price alone is not working. I think people are looking for some relief from their problems, yes, even escape. Maybe we can focus on some of the airline's destinations—places where people can relax and have some fun. And we can point out how Regis employees are doing everything they can to get the customer to those points of interest as quickly and comfortably as possible."

Silence, at first. Then, around the room, others started voicing their opinions. Most felt that Laura made some good points, and, if they didn't agree with her, they at least were sharing their views. Before the meeting ended, several team members were discussing ways to incorporate Laura's ideas into a new business presentation. When it was all over, Sumner Grady went over to Laura and complimented her for energizing the meeting with her ideas.

When she returned to her desk, Laura couldn't wait to tell Scotty how well she had done; she called him on the phone. "Wonderful" was his first reaction to the news. "Let me call you back. I'm on my way to see an important client."

"Oh, that's alright," she said. "I'll fill you in later. I'll bring the wine."

Laura met twenty-seven-year-old Scotty Brown at an advertising awards banquet. He was one of the judges. Married once briefly, he immediately impressed her as a handsome, smart, take-charge guy who would be one great catch for someone, especially someone who needed some direction and order in her life. She was hopeful that she eventually would be that someone.

But for now their commitment to each other was confined mainly to a shared Upper West Side studio apartment. They regarded their apartment as a temporary cohabitation, until one of them latched onto a ring farther up the executive ladder.

Scotty, a production assistant at a sales promotion company, had ambitions of starting his own business someday. A student of hot marketing trends, he wanted to set up a company that sold private-label cleaning products to nursing homes and hospitals. It was like Laura to offer her help in making Scotty's dream come true. She promised to use her creative abilities to promote the firm, once it was established. In her idle moments, which were rare, she would think up names and slogans for Scotty's company to be.

Their life began to follow a familiar pattern soon after they began living together. Most of the time, it was work, work, work interrupted by a nice dinner with some moderately priced wine (no dessert, please) and, later, passionate but brief sex. As busy and predictable as it was, they enjoyed their life together, especially the torrid, albeit abbreviated, lovemaking.

If there was a problem, it was Laura's growing curiosity about the parents she never knew. It started out as a minor irritation for Scotty, but when he saw how passionate she was becoming about what happened to them, he became increasingly annoyed. "Oh, come on, Laura. Let it go! How much more do you need to know?" he'd bristle before catching himself and kissing her on the lips to soften the blow. To his way of thinking, her quest for the truth about something that happened more than two decades ago was a wasted effort, and it cut into their time to plan and build a bright future together. To Laura, however, it was a detour in her life she simply had to make.

Laura was interested in learning as much as she could about her parents for as long as she could remember. *Who were they? What were they like? What happened to them?* When she was a girl growing up, Aunt Sally answered few of her questions. All she knew for a long time was that her mother, a beautiful woman, had died suddenly and was "in heaven with the Lord," and her father, a tall, handsome man, was so distraught after her death he went away, far away.

The more bits of information she picked up, the more she wanted to know. Soon, whenever she saw a tall, handsome man walking toward her in the street, the girl wondered, "Are you my father?" Once, a man she was eyeing stopped and said, "Do I know you, young lady?" Embarrassed, she shook her head and said, "I don't think so." Another time, a man gave her a flirtatious wink when she was staring at him. She soon stopped staring.

One of young Laura's biggest treats was visiting her maternal grandparents in New Jersey. She used to see Eve and Jesse Ames two or three times a year, which were never enough either for her or for her grandparents. Laura loved hearing them tell about what it was like when they first moved to New Jersey and began careers as teachers while rearing two children. She especially enjoyed the tales about Aurora, her mother. Sometimes the stories seemed to make Aunt Sally, who had been very close to her sister, very emotional, and she had to walk out of the room, but Laura soaked up every detail.

Laura liked everything she had come to know about her mother, including her personality, toughness, and sense of humor. "Oh, she had many friends and suitors," Mrs. Ames boasted. "She was named queen of the senior prom, you know."

Occasionally, Laura's grandparents would have a nice word to say about her father, but, unless the story forced them, they didn't draw him into the conversation. He was a gentleman, friendly and polite, Mr. Ames once noted. "We used to love the stories he told about Hollywood," Mrs. Ames said on another occasion. "You wouldn't believe some of the things that go on there."

After her grandparents died, Laura continued to pepper her aunt and uncle with questions about her parents, but they didn't give her many new answers. Laura was grateful for every morsel of information she received, but it was never enough.

It was only when she was 17 and hospitalized in Pennsylvania that she demanded the whole truth. She was recovering from a concussion and a broken collar bone, the result of a car accident on a nature outing with friends. In pain and not knowing the extent of her injuries, she turned to Aunt Sally and Uncle Roger and said, "Please, I need to know now. What happened to my mother? What happened to my father?" Carefully choosing their words, they told her about the murder, the suspicions that followed, and her father's decision to run away and leave his baby daughter with them. Laura wept, quietly, openly, without making any judgments.

5

THE BRIGHT CASINO LIGHTS FAR BEHIND HIM now, Lorne Bennett drove over ever-darkening roads to the street where he lived. Heading the car up the steep driveway that led to his one-level, rented house, Lorne was surprised by the flashes of light coming from his living room. He bolted out of the car and ran toward the front door. Suddenly remembering he had forgotten to turn off the TV when he left the house earlier, he stopped, heaved a sigh of relief, and reached in his pocket for his keys. They were not there.

He turned and went back to the car. Opening the front passenger door, he leaned over the seat and pulled the keys out of the ignition. But as he stepped back on to the driveway, he realized he had left the car in neutral, not park, and the parking brake was not engaged. The car started rolling backward.

Lorne slipped and scraped his knees against the driveway as he desperately tried to jump back into the car and stop it. When the car began rolling down the hill, he tried to catch up with it, but couldn't. The moving force of the vehicle was too strong, and the car picked up speed. Lorne was frantic as the distance between him and the car widened.

"Watch out, watch out!" he shouted to anyone in the way.

A helpless feeling left him shaking all over. It was as if he were chasing a runaway train.

Night had settled on the quietness of the Valley. People were home, relaxing after another long, hot day. But as the shouts outside grew louder, many ran to their windows, in time to see a cadre of concerned citizens running down the road followed by a tall man limping along as fast as he could. Some residents left their homes and joined the runners, still not sure they knew what or whom they were chasing.

Near a busy intersection, the car veered into a construction site and, after rumbling past two partially constructed prefabs, sideswiped a pile of gravel, backed into some wood pilings, turned around, and came to a scraping stop over the edge of a newly constructed swimming pool.

Trembling all over, Lorne fell to his knees, as if in prayer. No one seemed to be hurt, and he was glad for that, but a police car was whining nearby. Now the private, little world he had tried so hard to conceal was about to be opened up for the whole world to see, and he was terrified.

The phone rang, and Billy Volpe picked it up. He introduced himself, but there was no return greeting from the Mesa editor on the other end. Billy began nodding in agreement, taking some notes on whatever paper he could find. "Sure, Taylor, I'll get right there," he said, and hung up. Alex was already putting on her sneakers.

"Where're we going?" she asked.

"A car went out of control near Apache Boulevard," he explained, "but you're not going anywhere."

"Ah, dad! Maybe I can pick up some buzz."

"Not this time. It's late. I'll tell you all about it when I get home."

The phone rang again, and Alex snapped it up this time. "Oh hi, Trudi."

Billy gave his daughter a playful wave goodbye and charged

out the front door, his camera bag slung over his shoulder. He tapped his back pocket to make sure his notebook was there.

Lorne nervously watched the attention building around the accident he created. Years of running and hiding had taken him to places as scattered as Mexico and Bali, not to mention some of the remotest towns in the United States. Most of the time, he had felt reasonably safe. There were a few times he thought he was recognized, but either the sighting was fleeting and fizzled or it seemed threatening enough for Lorne to move to a new residence. If he worked, it was merely to keep himself fit and it was usually in a job not likely to draw a lot of attention, such as landscaper or construction worker. If he really needed money, he'd dip into funds transferred to bank accounts he had set up—just before he fled—with a couple of friends back East. He'd merely contact Russ Chaney, who owned a West Side bar, or Richie Frisco, a boyhood buddy, and ask him to send whatever he needed.

After his many travels, Lorne thought he had found the perfect haven in the desert. While his Arizona neighbors were busy at work or enclosed in the cool confines of their stucco homes, he was resuming something closer to a normal life. But, just to be sure, he usually did not stray too far from his modest rental. When he was not making meals he remembered from the fine restaurants he had frequented in his heyday, he was reading, listening to jazz music, surfing the Internet, or writing and tearing up letters to his daughter. Occasionally, under disguises he painstakingly created, he would venture out to a store to buy something he needed, or just to be with people.

Now here he was, unintentionally risking exposure to the outside world. For what? Because he forgot to put his car into parking gear? What an incredibly stupid and frustrating turn of events! Within two minutes, not one but two patrol cars were on the scene. Soon a local news reporter arrived, his camera clicking away at everything in sight, while a growing group of curious onlookers clustered around the Camry hanging over the newly built pool. Overhead, a helicopter paused briefly over the flashing lights below, then moved on.

Lorne could not believe the drawing power of what he considered a minor accident, albeit one that could have been disastrous. Now, either he would be found out and arrested or he would have to retreat as quickly as possible. The prospect of life on the run again was very real, and the thought made him sick. But what choice did he have?

Trying to keep his face hidden in the shadows, he explained the events leading up to the accident to a police officer. Nearby, a reporter was taking notes as quickly as he could. Later, while he spoke with another officer, the same reporter was snapping pictures from various angles, sometimes changing cameras as he did. Lorne was surprised by the number of photos Billy Volpe was taking.

"Hey, do you need so many pictures?" Lorne shouted, a slow panic descending on him. "It's only a damn car accident. No one got hurt."

Billy looked down at Lorne's pants which were torn to shreds at the knees. "Just doing my job, Mr. Fox. My editor is a stickler about taking lots of pictures. Can't get enough of them."

Lorne was surprised the reporter knew his name, or what he called himself, but then remembered that the reporter had overheard his conversation with the police, which provided some salient facts he needed for his story.

"Don't worry," said Billy. "Lucky if the paper uses one photo."

"Which paper is that?" asked Lorne.

Billy told him. "I'll send you a copy," he added.

"Don't bother," said Lorne.

Billy shrugged his shoulders, then moved over to photograph the Camry over the edge of the swimming pool.

Lorne shook his head, annoyed. By and large, he had gotten along well with journalists over his career, but there was always the exception. And, of course, Aurora was there in the past to help him stay calm and avoid confrontation. "Make nice, Kid," she would often advise him. "Make nice." And he did.

It was almost two hours before a tow truck operator managed

to lift the Camry off the pool's edge. Fortunately, the under-frame of the car did not appear to be severely damaged, and the mechanic was able to get the car running again. By then everyone had gone, except Lorne. On his way home he knew what he had to do. It was an old, trusted plan he did not expect to put into motion again, or at least for a long time. He had to get out of town.

It didn't take him long to pack a couple of bags and a carry-on, limp into his car, and drive off into the desert night.

6

Back home, Billy began working on the runaway car assignment. He thought he had a nice little story, perhaps one or two usable photos, but that's about it. Just in case, he would put together a package of materials with several photos, including one showing the Camry's owner talking to the police while the car sat on the edge of the pool.

As he was reviewing a group of pictures, Alex came into the room and looked over his shoulder. A bottle of cranberry juice in one hand, she examined the photos, one by one, "Not much of a story, eh, dad?"

"You never know what editors are looking for," he responded. "Might be a slow day."

She pointed to a photo of the car over the edge of the pool. "That one's not bad."

He nodded.

"Hmm," she said as if she discovered something. She was looking at the photo of the man talking to a police officer. "Is that the car owner?"

"Yes."

"Looks like he scraped his knees. Hmm ... he looks familiar. I've seen him someplace."

She squinted for a better look.

"Maybe you met him in Wal-Mart or Walgreens?"

"Noooooooo. Someplace else. Take a closer look."

Billy picked up the camera and moved the viewing screen as close as possible to his line of vision. "He looks like Clint Eastwood."

"Very funny."

He knew better than to take her too lightly when she was trying to be serious. "Look, Alex, I need more information about the accident. Based on my first impression, I don't think Mr. Fox loves reporters, but I'm going to chance it. First thing in the morning, I'm going over to his place and have a talk with him. Want to come? Maybe I can get a better read on your mystery man."

"You bet."

Billy was not surprised to see that Alex was ready, as promised, the next morning. Slung over her shoulder was the pink purse she carried almost everywhere important she went. In it were some of her most valuable possessions, including a picture of her parents, a memorial prayer card from grandpa Volpe's wake, and a hairbrush, small tube of suntan cream, and a cell phone. Just in case, she also carried a jar of Vicks VapoRub, Band-Aids, and tissues, along with some throat lozenges.

When they arrived at Peter Fox's house, Billy noted that there was no car in the driveway. It was early Saturday, and he thought Fox would not likely be going anywhere after the accident. But then maybe the car is in the repair shop and he's home waiting for the job to be finished.

Billy knocked on the front door. No answer. Alex looked through the window. She shook her head. "Don't see anyone." Billy walked toward the back of the house. "Mr. Fox! Mr. Fox!" he called out. Silence.

On a stone path, Alex reached over and picked up a baby's pink sock with white zigzags. She looked around for a mate but couldn't find any, then shoved the loner into her purse.

From the patio in the back, Billy picked up a small, gold-plated key that glittered in the sun and handed it to Alex. It also went into her bag for safekeeping.

Squinting through the sliding glass door, Billy could see no one in the kitchen. Everything looked orderly, as far as he could see. "Come on, Alex. Let's go."

"It's crazy, dad. A man goes for a ride in his car after having a bad accident?"

"Maybe he went for a container of milk or a six-pack or something," he suggested.

"Maybe ... but he must be hurting. Didn't he scrape his legs?" she asked.

They waited outside the house for a half-hour, but Fox didn't return.

Billy started up the car. "I just want to check the distance between the house and the scene of the accident. Other than that, I think I have enough to write up a nice, little money-maker."

When they got home, Billy went right to work at the computer. Since no one was badly hurt, he decided to tell the story with a light touch. After laboring over the lead paragraph, he reread what he had written.

An automobile suffering from heat exhaustion after a long day in the sun went berserk and made a beeline for a neighbor's swimming pool.

No. Too cute. He decided to play it straight.

Three paragraphs later, Billy dug his cell phone out of his jeans and dialed Fox's number. No answer. *How long does it take to buy a six-pack?* When he finished the article, he phoned Fox one more time, again without success. Then he e-mailed the story along with three photos to Taylor Reed. Twenty minutes later the editor responded:

Good story, but wonder why you didn't take a lighter approach. Have room for one pix, the crowd shot. T

Editors! Billy e-mailed him back.

Good choice. By the way, what do you know about Peter Fox? B

The editor's response indicated he had done a little snooping of his own.

Not too much. In area for about five years. Lives alone. House rented. Car paid in full. Google had nothing. T
    A mystery man without a past?

7

After hanging up the phone, Billy poured himself a glass of Chianti left over from the night before and walked into the living room. Alex was curled up on an old, lumpy armchair doing something she loved to do, watching an old movie, or what was old in her mind.

"What're you watching?" he asked.

Alex didn't answer right away, then felt obliged. *"Death with a Twist."*

"Saw it. About a man in a wheelchair who's accused of committing all these murders."

"Shh, don't tell me anymore, dad."

"The man is played by what's-his-name ..."

"Lorne Bennett."

"Right. He played a lot of Westerns when he first started, but then branched out into other stuff. I remember this one movie ..."

Alex squirmed in her chair. Suddenly, her eyes lit up. It was as if she discovered a cure for the common cold. "Dad, that's Peter Fox!" she shouted.

Billy nodded, wondered. *Why did he change his name?*

Early next morning, they headed for the local library. It was

Alex's idea to see what they could learn about Lorne Bennett from the volumes of books on the movie industry.

Billy had heard about the actor, and as a boy he had seen some of his movies. Handsome devil, fine actor, but there was something else about the man, something he did, a vague memory that so far refused to rise to the surface.

In the arts and entertainment section, Billy and Alex pulled down several reference books and anthologies from the shelves and began riffling through them. Then there it was, a photo of a tall, sinewy man in his thirties, his arms around a beautiful, young woman. Both were smiling. The caption read:

Picture of Happiness: Lorne Bennett is shown with his wife Aurora after finishing his latest film, The Accidental Missionary. *Bennett, who cut his teeth in Westerns, has been trying new roles, including double agent, wheelchair murderer, and now missionary. If you have trouble recognizing him from picture to picture, it's because he's a master of disguises. Mr. Bennett once told a Hollywood reporter that he never wanted to be anything more than a good character actor.*

The blurb went on to explain that the recently married Bennetts lived in Los Angeles and New York City, concluding: *True to his roots, The West Side Kid regularly visits his old pals in Hell's Kitchen on Manhattan's West Side, where he grew up.*

Alex seemed puzzled when Billy finished reading the caption. "Why did he change his name to Peter Fox? And what's he doing here?"

"I was wondering the same thing," said Billy. He smelled a big story.

"Don't know about you, dad, but I'm hungry," said Alex." I feel like a tuna wrap."

"Sounds good."

On the way home, Billy stopped at Blockbusters and picked up a DVD of *The Accidental Missionary*. It proved to be an uneven film, not very remarkable except for Lorne

Bennett's brilliant performance as a bumbling missionary

who saves a town from a flood. Alex, who laughed every time Lorne's character, the Reverend Foxworthy, came on the scene, lost interest at the end when the flood began and the film turned serious.

Her curiosity piqued by what she had just seen, she smeared some peanut butter on four Ritz crackers, poured herself a glass of 2% milk, and sat down at the computer desk in the den. Determined to find out as much as she could about Mr. Bennett or Mr. Fox, whoever he was, she glanced at a wide selection of Web offerings before coming across a news article that startled her. "Dad, come here. You have to see this!"

The news story was headlined "Do You Know Where Lorne Bennett Is?" The story was dated a month before. They both began reading:

Twenty-two years ago today, Aurora Bennett was shot to death in her apartment in a charming East Side section of New York City. She was found on the floor of her living room, one bullet in her chest. It appeared that she had died while crawling to a nearby room where her four-month-old daughter Laura was fast asleep.

The story went on:

A person of interest whom police are now calling the prime suspect—Aurora's husband, the famous actor Lorne Bennett—went missing shortly after the murder and is still on the loose. Over the years, several people reported spotting the man in places as far away as Bali, but the sightings, according to New York police, were never confirmed. The case appears to be as cold as a mackerel on ice, but cold-case detectives said they have not given up and are continuing their "relentless" search for the actor known as The West Side Kid. A reward of $100,000 has been posted for information leading to Bennett's arrest.

"Yeah, it's coming back to me now," said Billy, brushing his dark brown hair from his forehead. "I was only a kid at the time, but it was a big story."

After providing some background on Bennett, the article noted that police were blamed for not moving faster to bring him in for questioning. Then it added:

Several days after the murder, newspapers began raising

suspicions about Bennett's alibi. He had told police he was out walking alone after a night of drinking with some of his West Side pals, and when questioned about the nasty cut on the side of his head, he said he tripped and fell somewhere on Forty-Second Street. Police were able to confirm that Lorne was, indeed, at the pub where he said he was, but not his whereabouts afterward. Not a single witness came forward to support his alibi.

According to the article, there were reports that Aurora and Lorne Bennett had engaged in heated arguments, sometimes in public, in the past few months. In fact, a close friend of Aurora's told police that she knew for a fact that the Bennetts had a big blowup the day of the murder. The story then took a sensational turn:

A week after the funeral, his baby daughter in his arms, Bennett went to see his sister-in-law Sally Kent at her home in Queens and asked her to mind the child so he could spend a couple of days sorting things out. It seemed like a reasonable request, she later told reporters, so she agreed to watch the baby. Sally was close to her sister and happy to help, as was her husband Roger, a police officer and long-time friend of the family.

When the childless couple agreed to watch the baby, they had no idea they were embarking on a relationship that would last more than two decades, according to the article. The first inkling the Kents had that something had gone wrong was when Bennett called a couple of days later and said he was not coming back. Sounding very agitated and emotional, he told them he had no choice. It was flee or go to prison.

When the media got wind that Bennett had run away, they started speculating that he was helped in his flight by a coterie of his West Side friends, but this could not be confirmed, according to the article. It concluded by noting that Sally and Roger Kent embraced the newest member of their household.

They did everything in their power to give the child a good, stable home. Laura Bennett, who had recently launched a career in advertising, refused to comment on the story except to say that she had always been interested in learning more about her parents.

At the same time, she praised the Kents for being there when she needed them.

Billy took a gulp of wine. "Wow!"

"Yeah, Wow!" Alex agreed.

PART 2

THE INNOCENT PIT BULL

8

THERE WAS SOMETHING ABOUT THE WAY everyone talked about her father.

"I don't think what he did was right, running off like that," Aunt Sally told Laura one day. "But he was always a gentleman, and I know my sister loved your father, and as far as I know he loved her back. Isn't that right, Roger?"

"As far as I know," he replied.

News clippings were confusing. Some media reports called Lorne Bennett a brilliant but hard drinking and insecure movie star who shot his wife, point-blank, after a series of heated arguments. Others painted him as an immature, irresponsible new father who "abandoned" his baby daughter with in-laws after he killed his wife. Still others focused on Lorne Bennett, the compassionate and generous man who was involved in various charitable organizations and who had helped many people from his old neighborhood when they were in need.

It just didn't add up. Laura began to wonder whether the man she never knew could have killed her mother. To clarify some of the events leading up to and following the murder, she decided to see what the official records had to say.

On a park bench not far from her office one afternoon, Laura pulled out her cell phone and dialed a local police precinct. A sergeant at the desk referred her to a detective group working on cold case files downtown. In turn, a detective in that group informed her that the Aurora Bennett case was still active, but there were no new developments.

"We'll contact you if there's anything new to report," said Bud Turner, the lead detective on the case. "You know, there are thousands of unsolved murders out there and we're only a small group with limited funds. We do the best we can. Nothing would please us more than to give you closure. You let us know if you hear anything, okay?"

Still not satisfied, Laura took the next step, sending long, impassioned letters and short, follow-up e-mails to the police commissioner, the district attorney, and the mayor, all of whom replied with brief, civil messages offering assurances that their staffs were "looking into the matter" and thanking her for her interest

Disheartened but not defeated, she again called Detective Turner, who mentioned the "unconfirmed sightings" of her father. It was something, but far from satisfying. A new round of phone calls to key officials followed. Gradually, Laura was becoming well known within police and official city circles.

"It's that innocent pit bull who's looking for her father," announced a staff member in the cold files unit whenever he transferred Laura's call to Detective Turner.

The bits of information picked up here and there only encouraged Laura to continue her investigation. Sometimes she felt she was getting closer to the real story. It was two, small steps forward and one, big step backwards—or so it seemed—and the end was never in sight.

Then, one day she called Bud Turner, who caught her by surprise. He told her he was retiring from the police department.

"It's time," he said, "Twenty-five years on the job is enough. But at the same time I'll miss it."

"Wish you lots of luck," said Laura. "Any idea who'll replace you?"

"No, not yet," he replied. "Your mother's case was very important to me. It was my first big case as a detective, and I'll pass on whatever I know to the person who replaces me. Nothing would please me more than to see this case come to an end."

"Me, too."

"I don't know how to say this without hurting your feelings, but if we picked up your father today, it would be over just like that," he said, snapping his fingers.

"Sounds as if you believe my father had something to do with my mother's murder."

"There's a lot of circumstantial evidence against him," Turner argued. "And if your father had nothing to do with it, why did he run away?"

"I'm not convinced he did it," Laura sat flatly. "There's got to be someone out there who knows something we haven't heard before. Maybe a friend he confided in."

"Your father's closest friend, as far as I know, was Richie Frisco, one of his West Side buddies," he revealed. "We've been talking to him, on and off, for years; if he knows anything, he's not talking."

"Maybe I'll try ..."

"I wouldn't advise it," he warned. "This guy's old school, tough as nails, with the rap sheet to prove it. He's an ex-con with a manslaughter conviction."

"And he was my father's closest friend," she added.

Laura was both nervous and excited as she prepared to meet Frisco the following evening. He had sounded delighted to see her when she phoned him and arranged to meet him at a café on Ninth Avenue.

"It's hopeless. I can't do eyeliners," she groaned as she looked in a mirror on her desk at work.

"Maybe you could if your damned hands weren't shaking so much," suggested Anita, another member of the late-night office brigade.

Laura broke out into tears.

"Oh, come on," said Anita. "You don't need that crap on your eyes anyway. Anyone ever tell you that you have beautiful eyes?"

Laura drew in a deep breath and began applying the makeup again.

"You want me to go with you?" asked Anita, who had been kept aware of Laura's search for information about her parents.

"No, thanks. I don't know why I'm so nervous," said Laura.

"Does Scotty know where you're going?"

"No."

"Maybe that's why."

"I can't tell him. He doesn't want to know anything," said Laura. "And he doesn't want me to keep trying to find out."

"I know."

"He thinks I'm crazy to keep going over it," Laura went on. "The past is the past, he says. Forget about it. Keep your eye on our future, he tells me. I do, I really do, Anita. He thinks I'm crazy."

"Maybe you are. Maybe we're all a little nuts," said Anita, trying to lighten the mood.

Laura finished applying the makeup.

"You have to do what you think is right," said Anita.

Laura got up from her desk. "Yeah, thanks. Wish me luck."

"Watch your ass!"

It was getting dark when Laura reached the cafe. Inside, the staff was making the transformation for the late-night crowd. Most of the pre-theater diners were gone now, on their way to their long-anticipated Broadway shows. All but two of the tables were empty. At one table sat three young women who were raising their wine glasses to celebrate someone's divorce. Another table, way in the back, was the exclusive domain of a short, corpulent man in his late fifties who was tearing apart a sparerib. Surmising that the sparerib eater was the one she wanted to see, Laura headed for the rear of the restaurant, attracting the eyes of a couple of neighborhood regulars at the bar on the way.

"Hi, Mr. Frisco?" she inquired, bending over slightly, as she did whenever she felt self-conscious about her height. He looked up, returning one more eaten rib to his plate. "I'm Laura, Laura Bennett."

He smiled broadly and rose from the table, moving gracefully for a big man. After wiping his mouth and hands on his napkin, he hugged her and kissed her on the cheek. "Geez, I can't believe it's little Laura all grown up. You look just like your dad. Please sit down."

"I heard a lot about you, Mr. Frisco," she said.

"Most of it good, right?"

"Well, actually it was, most of it."

"If you're talkin' about that manslaughter thing, he asked for it. He smacked my kid across the face for sittin' on his bomb, this old Chevy, and he came at me with a wrench when I went to return the favor."

"Well," she went on hesitantly, "I don't want to take up too much of your time or interrupt your dinner. I just want to ask a few questions, Mr. Frisco."

"Please. Call me Richie."

"Okay. Richie."

"Good." He reached over and patted her reassuringly on the hand. "Look, you're not cuttin' into my time or my dinner," he continued. "It's a pleasure and honor to finally meet Lorney Bennett's little girl. Now, please, eat somethin'. Best spareribs in town here."

"Oh, no thanks."

"I insist."

She looked down at his plate of uneaten ribs. "Well, maybe I'll have just one of yours."

Frisco waved to a passing waiter. "Hank, Hank, bring a plate of ribs for the lady, please."

"Right away, Richie."

"Wait ... how about somethin' to drink?"

"I'll have a Bud Light ... and a Coke," she said.

"Must be thirsty," smiled Frisco, with a shrug.

"Good people here," he continued, pointing to the restaurant owner and the staff. "All neighborhood people," he explained, making it clear that he "wouldn't be here if they weren't." He also noted with some regret that "the West Side is changin' faster than you can say 'Hell's Kitchen,'" and "most of the old-timers either moved out or are dead, whatever. Know what I mean?"

"Where does my dad fit in?" Laura asked.

"I guess he's in the 'whatever' group," Frisco replied. After a pause, he went on to explain that he and her father went back a long way together. They hung out together on the streets, they played on the same hockey and basketball teams, and, yes, they sometimes got into trouble together. "He was a pistol, always dreamin' up crazy, fun things to do."

He continued, "I remember when your father was just a snot-nosed kid. You kind of felt sorry for him, hoppin' from relative to relative after his mother died, but he never let on he had troubles of any kind. We were very close, Lorney and me. My father was never around much, either."

"Did you stay in touch with my father after he became an actor?"

"Oh, sure, Lorney was like that. His friends—and family, of course—always came first. Whenever he was in town, he stopped by. You may not know this, but he helped a lot of people in the neighborhood. A few bucks to this one, a few bucks to that one, includin' me. I am eternally full of gratitude."

The spareribs came, and Laura quickly realized how hungry she was. She attacked them with a fork and knife, not very easily. "They taste better when you pick them up in your hands, sweetie," he said. She took his suggestion. "Great ribs," she concluded. Frisco gave her a quick told-you-so nod.

"Now how can I help you?" he finally asked.

Laura thought a moment. "What do you remember about the night my mother died?"

"Well, I was with your father in Russ Chaney's Bar," he replied. "He was a little down that night. Had a big fight with the old lady—your mom, that is. We just talked and talked, the bunch of us. We all tried to make him laugh. The stories and jokes were flyin' all over the place. I mean he would have done the same for any of us. About ten-thirty or so, he just got up, said good-bye, and walked out, by himself. I don't know where he went or what he did after that."

"Was he drunk when he left?"

"He'd hoisted a few, but he could hold his own with anybody."

She sighed before asking her next question. "Do you think he killed my mom?"

There was no hesitation in Richie's reply. "No! I know your father." Then, after a second or two, he added, "Look, you never know what any person will do in anger or in pain or if he went crazy. He liked his good times, that's for sure, but I don't believe in my heart he did that terrible thing. In case you didn't know, he loved your mom too much. He is—I mean, was—a good guy who never forgot where he came from."

"You said 'is.' Do you know where my father is now?"

"I wish I could tell you, but I don't know. People like that are always on the move. All I can tell you is that if the police or the FBI knew where he was, they'd haul him back and lock him up and throw away the keys."

Richie watched as Laura fought back tears.

"Look, sweetie, I'm not goin' to bullshit—sorry!—bullcrap you. I wish I could say I know for sure, with proof, that he absolutely, positively, didn't kill your mom, because that's what the cops want to hear. All I know is, in my heart, he didn't do it, and I'm tellin' you this, not because it'll make you feel good. I'm tellin' you because it's true."

He reached over and gently held her hand. Then, he said, "Don't worry, sweetie. I'll help you find answers. I got some spies in the can—I mean, prison—and if they can sniff out anything, they will."

"Thanks, Mr. Frisco ... Richie."

"Now, how about some dessert?

She hesitated. Scotty was probably grinding his teeth now, she thought; he did that whenever he was angry. "Oh, no thanks. I really have to go."

Laura was wrung out by the time she got home. Scotty was ready to pounce. When she entered the apartment, he leapt off the tan leather sofa they called their "love seat," where they spent many nights together, and rammed his hands in the pockets of his jeans. He tried to disguise his rage. "Where've you been?"

"I told you I'd be working late," she reminded him.

"It's almost ten-thirty," he said, stealing a glance at the sunburst clock on the wall.

"I had things to do after work," she said.

"Christ, Laura! That's not acceptable! Were you visiting a sick friend in the hospital? Did your uncle have a heart attack? Were you in a car accident? Did you stop in Duane Reade for shampoo? Tell me anything, but, please, don't tell me you had 'things to do.' "

"Alright, I met someone. I met someone I thought had a lead on my father." She went on to explain her conversation with Richie Frisco. Trying to make Scotty see the importance of the meeting, she said, "He was a friend of my father's. He helped fill in some of the blanks about that night, and he promised to let me know if he hears anything else. He has people in the can, I mean prison, who can give him information, for God's sake."

Scotty sat down at the end of the sofa, Laura on the bed. He heaved a deep sigh. "When is it going to stop? When are you going to let it go, Laura?"

"I can't, Scotty."

"It was twenty-two years ago. It's over."

"As far as I'm concerned, it's not over. My father is still out there, or at least I think he is. And if he isn't, I want to know what happened to him. Is that asking too much?"

"Yes. It's taking too much of our time."

"Oh, come on, Scotty, I don't expect you to help me do what I have to do, but I thought you'd understand why I'm doing it—and I didn't think you'd mind waiting," she added.

His response was slow, deliberate. "If you mean waiting to get married, I don't mind waiting for that. But I do mind waiting for you to come home, not knowing where you are, that whole secret life of yours."

"I'm sorry you feel that way, Scotty, but there's nothing secret about what I'm doing."

"Oh, come on."

"I always told you what I was doing."

"Yeah, like you did tonight."

She searched for the right words. "Maybe we'd better cool it for tonight."

Scotty flattened the throw pillow behind his head and stretched out on the sofa. "Fine with me."

9

THE NEXT MORNING, LAURA WOKE UP AND reached over to give Scotty a good-morning hug. He wasn't there. In fact, when she jumped out of bed and looked around, he was nowhere to be found. Apparently, he had gotten up earlier than usual, breaking their routine, and darted off to work. Without giving her a wake-up tap. Without the usual morning banter. Without a good-bye kiss.

Laura, who was usually quick to forget and to forgive, had thought the previous night's argument would be a fading memory by morning. It wasn't, at least not for Scotty, it appeared. Laura was hurt by Scotty's reaction, and miffed, as she tried to get ready for work. She didn't care if her clothes matched or whether her makeup was applied correctly.

Rushing out the door, she caught the elevator just as the doors were closing and was headed down to the lobby when she realized she had forgotten her briefcase. It was back upstairs to retrieve the briefcase, catch the elevator, out the front door and into the August sun.

She was almost running now, heading toward the corner where she usually caught a cab to work. Then—Wham!—a large piece of scaffolding from a nearby building that was under reconstruction suddenly came crashing down onto the sidewalk less than ten feet away from her. "Geez, you see that!" shouted an old man walking his dog across the street. A plump woman, her eyes as frightful as an owl's, rushed across the street to Laura's side.

"My God! You alright, lady?" Laura, paralyzed for a moment, nodded. Charlie, her doorman, came running up the street and put his arm on her shoulder. "You okay, Ms. Bennett?"

Laura nodded again and stared at the pieces of scaffolding splattered on the sidewalk. Then, blocking the sun with her hand, she gazed up at the building that was getting the facelift. She thought she saw someone climbing into one of the windows on the top floor.

"You could've been killed!" said the plump woman, who was looking around nervously. "Someone call the cops," shouted the man with the dog. Another woman pulled out a cell phone and started dialing. Laura looked at her watch. Her morning meeting would start in ten minutes. There was no time to wait for the police and tell them what had happened. She had to get to work. Except for being badly shaken, she was unhurt. Hailing a cab on the corner, Laura wondered what else could go wrong.

The office is many things to many people, but to Laura it meant one thing on most days: a chance to do something she loved to do—be creative in an atmosphere where good work, camaraderie, and fun were encouraged. Today, however, after the hellish start to her morning, she didn't feel like being very creative, productive, or sociable. It was all she could do to concentrate on what her colleagues were saying at the interdepartmental meeting. There was no way she could shake the chilling sound and sight of those thick, jagged planks of wood crashing on the sidewalk so close to her. Was it an accident, or was someone trying to send her a message, or worse?

Laura, who usually managed to recover from her initial stage fright, was ashen and trembling when it was her turn to present. Her job was to explain the creative strategy behind the new Today women shoes fall campaign. In a deliberate but clear voice, she showed the magazine ads to the group and answered a couple of questions, none difficult, thank heaven. When it was over, she breathed a sigh of relief and gathered up her things and headed back to her office, disappointed with her performance.

Anita caught up with her. "Tough audience, eh, babe?"

"Tough morning," Laura replied.

"Come on, let's get out of here."

At a little deli-restaurant across the street, Laura was reluctant to talk, but under Anita's not-so-gentle prodding, she told her everything, from the sparerib dinner with Richie Frisco to the argument with Scotty to her near-death experience with the falling scaffolding.

Anita shook her head in commiseration.

"Yeah, what next?" Laura commented.

Anita sprang out of a slight slouch. "Nothing. *Niente.* Zero. Don't talk like that!"

"I can't help it."

"Just chalk it up as a couple of rotten days."

"I can't."

"Why not?" asked Anita.

Laura took a sip of tea. "Because I have a feeling things are going to get worse, not better," she replied.

"Tell me about Richie Frisco," said Anita. "Were you happy with what he told you?"

"Yes. The man answered my questions as best as he could, and he's trying to help me." Laura paused, then added, "I don't know whether I should be telling you all this stuff. I'm afraid to involve you, Anita."

"Don't worry about it. I can take care of myself. If I can't, I have a cousin who collects serial-killer cards." Anita picked up the check. "Come on, let's do something uneventful. Let's go back to work."

Laura had four voice messages when she returned to her office. The first was from Sumner Grady, the creative director. "The campaign is a go except for a few minor changes. Come to my office at two-thirty. We'll discuss. Nice job this morning." She was surprised by the compliment.

The second message was from Aunt Sally. "Oh hi, honey. Haven't talked to you in a couple of days. Hope all's well with you and Scotty. We're fine. I just want to tell you about a phone call I got that concerns you. Call me when you get a chance." Laura could hear a whistling sound in the background, probably a tea kettle boiling, then someone, probably Uncle Roger, shouting, "Would you please shut that damn thing off?"

The third call was short and direct. "Hello, Ms. Bennett. This is Detective Rios. Please call me when you get a chance." He left his number.

On the fourth call, Laura heard only static and a disconnect click.

First on her callback list was Aunt Sally, who seemed excited to hear from her niece. "I just wanted to let you know that some man called," she relayed. "He wanted to speak to you and asked for your number. I didn't give it to him at first. But then he told me he had some important information about your father, and he wanted to make your life easier. I hope I did the right thing, but I gave him your number. It was this morning, about six o'clock. I was afraid the phone would wake up Roger. He has an afternoon shift."

"Did you give him my home number or office number?"

"Both."

Laura winced. "Did he give you his name?"

"No, but caller ID said West Side Demolition."

"Thanks, Aunt Sally. I'll drop by this weekend, if I can. Love you."

Laura checked her watch. There was a lot of work to be done, but she had to make another call. Detective Rios was not in the office, but she did find out that Carlos Rios had replaced Bud Turner on dozens of files, including the Aurora Bennett case. She left a message.

Next, Laura reached for the phone directory and found a listing for a West Side Demolition Company and dialed the number. A woman on the other end announced, "West Side Demolition. We build, too. May I help you?"

It was time for a little creativity—more accurately, a lie. "Oh, hi, this is the editor of *Building and Demolition Age.* I'm working on a story, and I'd like to speak to your owner or manager."

"That would be Ned Lacey. He's not here right now."

"Would you kindly spell his name?"

"That's L-A-C-E-Y."

"He's usually here between six and six-thirty every morning."

Bingo.

"I'll try to reach him then."

Twice more, in the afternoon, she tried to call Detective Rios, but he was either "unavailable" or "out on assignment." She'd try again.

10

THE CHERRY MAHOGANY TABLE WAS DECORATED with a candle centerpiece that was lit and two of their better place mats when Laura arrived home that evening. "Well, this is a surprise," she said, a lingering coolness in her voice. She hadn't heard from him all day.

Scotty placed a tuna salad platter on the table and began pouring the Zinfandel. "I thought we'd have something cold tonight," he said.

"Is this a guilt dinner?" she asked.

He stopped pouring. "Guilt? I have nothing to be guilty about."

Laura went to the sink and washed her hands. "Well, you did leave in a hurry this morning."

"I had an early meeting, remember?"

"No."

"I thought I told you."

"You told me lots of things, but not that."

"Oh, don't start again."

"You're the one who started it, Scotty. I'm sorry you don't understand what I'm doing."

"Yeah, I know. Do what you have to do," he said. "Why don't we just eat?"

"Good idea." They sat down at the table and began eating. Silence. He tried to break it. "How was your day?"

"Fine," she replied, not a whiff about the scaffolding incident.

"And the campaign?"

"It was approved."

"Oh, that's great," he said.

The phone rang, and Laura sprang up to answer it. When she learned that the caller was Detective Rios, she moved away from the dining area and sat on the bed.

"Oh hi, Detective," she began. "Yes, I know. We keep missing each other."

Scotty rose, picked up his plate, cleaned it off and placed it in the sink, then walked out the front door. Laura watched him leave the apartment and shook her head in disgust.

"I just want you to know that I'm replacing Bud Turner on the case," he said as if he were reading a prepared statement. "I plan to use every resource at my command to find your mother's killer and give you closure."

"Thank you, I appreciate that, Detective. I want you to know that I plan to do everything I can, too."

"I know you will, Ms. Bennett."

"For starters, I have some information that may interest you," Laura continued. She went on to tell him about her meeting with Richie Frisco.

"We know about Mr. Frisco," he jumped in. "We talked to him. His comments are on file."

"He believes my father didn't do it."

"We know what he believes."

Laura saw an opening for a question. "Where did my father say he was when my mother was murdered?"

Rios sighed, then recited what he knew. "He said he left the bar at around ten-thirty and walked around into late the next afternoon. The part about the bar checked out, but the rest of it couldn't be confirmed. As far as the gash on the side of his head, he said he fell on the sidewalk."

"What do you know about Ned Lacey?" asked Laura.

"Bad news," Rios replied. "He's managed to stay out of jail, but just. He's a dangerous character."

She thought about the planks of wood that came crashing down near her. The incident had occurred only that morning, but it seemed as if it happened a long time ago. She decided to say nothing about it to Rios. *He doesn't have to know everything! Besides, what could he do? Watch everything I do? Curtail my movements?*

"Please, Ms. Bennett, let the police handle the police work," he pleaded. "There are a lot of very nasty people out there who wouldn't think twice about harming you. Understand?"

"I do, and thanks for reminding me."

After she hung up, Laura decided to clean off the table. She had lost her appetite.

Laura didn't know how long she was sleeping after Scotty left. All she knew was that she was in total darkness when the phone rang. A glance at the luminous clock on a side table told her it was just past midnight. She picked up the phone and answered with a murky "Hello."

"Ms. Bennett?" The voice was low and throaty, almost unreal.

"Yes."

"Do yourself and your aunt and uncle a favor. Stop snooping around, and stay away from the cops. You could have been really hurt this morning."

"Who's this? Who's this?" The phone on the other end remained open for a few seconds, then click! The caller was gone.

Laura sat up at the edge of the bed, her heart beating crazily. *Oh, how I wish Scotty were here! WHERE IS HE?*

Fright soon gave way to anger, and she knew she would not be able to go back to sleep. She sprang up, plopped on the sofa, and snapped on the TV. Black-and-white scenes of the Soviet invasion of Berlin near the end of World War II came flitting by when a click was heard and the knob on the door began turning.

Laura froze momentarily, then opened the drawer of a nearby end table. Reaching for anything, she grabbed a flashlight and moved, cat-like, toward the entranceway and stopped. Whoever was trying to get in paused for a moment. Laura was trembling as she stood by the side of the doorway. The door knob began turning again, but very slowly, as if someone was trying not to arouse too much attention. As the door slowly opened, she raised the flashlight over her head, ready to strike the intruder. For a second, the light from the hallway blinded her, but when she recovered her sight, she recognized Scotty.

He raised his hands defensively. "Whoa! Is that any way to greet an old friend?"

Laura collapsed in his arms, sobbing. "Damn you! Where the hell were you?"

"I went to see my parents. I was watching the Mets game. Maybe I had too much wine. I fell asleep. The next thing, my father woke me up and told me to go home."

"He had to tell you to go home? Why did you leave in the first place? Dinner was sitting there on the table."

"I couldn't take it," he replied.

"So you just got up and left?"

"I was coming back."

"When? Why didn't you call me?" she wondered.

"I tried, but the line was busy," he said. "Who was calling you at midnight?"

"Geez, doesn't that tell you something? I mean, if someone is calling me at midnight, and it's not you ... Ah, what's the use of trying to explain? I'm going back to bed." Although she wouldn't admit it, Laura was comforted Scotty was home.

11

THE NEXT MORNING, WORRIED ABOUT A SUDDEN downpour, Laura hurried up the street to catch a cab for work. As she neared the construction site, she warily surveyed the upper levels of the building, saw no one, then stepped up her pace. Halfway up the block, the first raindrops began falling. She stopped, turned around to see if anyone was behind her, and opened her umbrella. As she did, she noticed a short, stocky man in a light blue jacket barreling toward her.

After yesterday's near-miss, she was not about to take any chances. She was almost running now. By the time she reached the corner, it was pouring, and the man in the light blue jacket had almost caught up to her. An intensity and determination in his eyes signaled danger.

Laura stepped into the rain-soaked street and hailed an oncoming cab. The man was close behind her as the taxi came to a sudden stop. With a magician's sleight of hand, Laura closed her umbrella, jumped in, and slammed the door. The man started pounding on the window. "Hey, want to share the cab?" he barked, almost out of breath.

"Crazies!" muttered the cabbie as he drove away.

Another time, Laura might have laughed at the incident, but not this morning. She was too tense and nervous.

When Laura arrived at her office, she found Anita sitting there, casually flipping through the pages of *New York* magazine. "Let's do lunch," said Anita, apparently sensing that her friend was troubled and not up for a heart-to-heart conversation right now.

"I can't," said Laura. "Big presentation this afternoon. I'll call you tonight."

"Bull! I'll pick you up at twelve o'clock," Anita insisted.

Laura agreed and logged on to check her messages. All clear, except for one unexpected note, from Detective Rios: "Why didn't you tell me about the scaffolding?"

Later that day, when she arrived at the Kents' home in Queens, Laura noticed that nothing had changed at the place where she grew up, and that was good; she needed that sense of stability and continuity in her life.

Her aunt and uncle had just finished dinner, and a plate was waiting for her at the dining room table.

"Sorry I'm late. Crazy day," she explained.

"Sit down," said Aunt Sally. "I hope you like tuna salad."

Laura didn't have the heart to tell her that tuna was on the previous night's menu. "Love it."

She got a good look at her aunt. Perhaps she was not as stunningly beautiful as her younger sister Aurora was, but Aunt Sally was a lovely woman. In her late fifties now, she had gray streaks in her short, brown hair, and new lines were beginning to branch out from the corners of her dark eyes. Like her sister, she was tall and lean, quick on her feet, but she was slightly more stooped in the way she carried herself.

So many nurturing moments came to mind whenever Laura thought about Aunt Sally. One, in particular, stood out. Laura was six years old and feverish with pneumonia. Uncle Roger was at work at the time. After trying everything she could to break the fever, Aunt Sally felt she had no other choice than to bundle up the girl and drive her to the emergency room in a snowstorm. It was a good thing, said the doctors. Three days later, the girl was back home.

"It's been, what, two weeks since we last saw you?" Roger began.

"Just about. What's new with you, Uncle Roger?"

"I'm almost at the finish line," he replied. "I signed some retirement papers today. I think I'm gone at the beginning of next year." His light blue eyes showed no emotion, as if he didn't want to make too much of it too soon, but then Uncle Roger was never a very emotional person. Always a muscular man who worked out regularly, he was putting on weight around the mid-section, which Laura noticed.

"That's great," she remarked.

To Laura, her aunt and uncle were a caring couple. While they were not likely to demonstrate their affections publicly, they usually made their feelings known, shielding each other—and Laura, of course—from any possible injury or pain. Only lately did they seem to bicker a little more, which Laura chalked up to something that comes with age. Generally, Uncle Roger deferred family decisions to Aunt Sally.

Family took precedence with her aunt ands uncle, and both seemed driven to do the right thing. Aunt Sally was involved in a host of activities in the local church, while Uncle Roger was determined to maintain his reputation as a good cop. Both were always ready to impart some lesson of life, which sometimes amused Laura. "We're the original Brady Bunch," she'd jokingly tell her friends.

Although her aunt and uncle never had children of their own, Laura felt she was always treated like one of the family. How many sacrifices did they make to get the young woman through college and into her own apartment? And weren't they always there when she needed someone to listen?

"How is your search going?" Uncle Roger asked Laura.

Both her uncle and aunt had known for some time that she had been contacting police and other municipal sources for information about her parents. Hesitantly—because she didn't want to worry them—she told them about her conversations with Richie Frisco and Detective Rios, but she didn't say anything about the scaffolding that almost struck her.

Laura's cell phone rang, and she reached into her bag to answer it. "Hello." Silence followed. Then, a gruff voice came on. "Like I told you, if you love your family, you'll stop asking questions now!"

Click.

"I think someone's trying to tell me to mind my own business," said Laura.

"Maybe that's not such a bad idea," said Uncle Roger. "Don't you agree, Sal?"

"Yes," Aunt Sally replied. "Now come on, you two. You must be starved, Laura."

PART 3

HAVE YOU SEEN THE LIONS?

12

THE RIDE NORTH SEEMED ENDLESS, MARKED BY
miles and miles of scorched earth, shrubs, and cactus stubs. As
morning dawned, Lorne could see the outline of a mountain range
rising majestically in the distance.

Lorne stopped at a desert-style convenience store along the
way and bought some coffee, a large bottle of water, and a bag of
nachos. Then, sitting on a clump of earth, he sipped his coffee, ate
his nachos and gazed at the mountains. It was the first time in a
long time he felt so alone.

He remembered how he felt back then ...

There was something special about growing up on the West
Side. For one thing, someone was always hanging around. It was a
phenomenon that lasted all year long, but was especially evident
in the summer. That's when the playgrounds and streets were
teeming with playing, laughing, fighting, and scheming kids. And
there was an order to all of the chaos.

Back then, unless you were a total outsider or newcomer,
each kid belonged to a particular group or gang, and each gang
was aligned to a particular street where the boys and girls lived
or gathered. The reputation of each gang varied, depending on

the age, background, and financial circumstances of its members. Some were tougher and more likely to get in trouble with police than others, and most were engaged in some form of sports activity. The gang was home away from home for most kids, including ten-year-old Lorne Bennett.

One cold November night, he watched with dread as one by one of his friends got up from the fire they made in a vacant lot on Eleventh Avenue and went home. Only Richie Frisco remained. Finally, he rose, brushed off his torn jeans, and announced that he had to go, too. "My mother's waitin' and my father will kill me if I get home after he does."

"Its still early, Richie," said Lorne, a touch of desperation in his voice. "Stick around. We'll talk. Hockey? Movies? Religion? Anything you want to talk about."

"Geez, I can't, Lorney. He'll murder me."

"Hey, want to sneak into a movie?"

"Nah, Lorney. Everyone else's gone home. Why don't you?"

"What for, Richie? My mother's ushering tonight."

"What about your dad?"

"My dad?" said Lorne. "Who's he? He works all night, two jobs, and he sleeps all day. I'm lucky if he says two words to me."

"Geez, I'm sorry, Lorney, but I gotta go ... See you tomorrow."

"Yeah, meet you in the playground."

Richie nodded and walked away.

"Right after school, okay?" Lorne shouted after him. "Bring your skates." He wasn't sure Richie had heard him

Lorne threw another piece of wood on the fire. He was in no hurry to get home. With both parents spending so much time working—his mother Irene cleaned offices in the afternoon and ushered in the theater at night and his father Larry held night jobs at a warehouse and as a watchman—Lorne felt he could come and go as he pleased. He seldom felt there would be consequences if he was out later than the other kids in the neighborhood.

By the time he got home, it was almost ten-thirty. Lorne was shocked to see his mother waiting for him. She had left work a little earlier because she wasn't feeling well.

"Do you have any idea what time it is, mister?" she demanded.

"Sorry, mama," he said.

"Where've you been?"

"Out, mama."

"You smell like fire."

"It was cold. We built a fire in the lot, and Richie Frisco brought some marshmallows."

"Were you smoking?"

"Oh, no, mama. I don't smoke. It's bad for you."

"You're such a good actor, Lorney. Go get yourself something to eat. I'm going back to bed. You're coming with me to the theater tomorrow night." It would be his first contact with Broadway.

A year later, his mother died unexpectedly of heart failure, and Lorne's world collapsed. When he wasn't moping around with his friends, he'd go off by himself and sit on the roof and gaze out over the city. More occupied and distant than ever, his father shuttled Lorne from relative to relative, sometimes for the night, sometimes for a few days, sometimes for a week or more. Aunt Rose, his mother's sister, finally pleaded with Larry to let Lorne stay longer with her. His father agreed, and Lorne's world began to take new shape.

One day, Aunt Rose, a widow and former teacher, handed him a book, *The Last of the Mohicans.*

"What's this?" asked Lorne.

"It's a book about a frontier scout and his Indian friend. Read it, you'll enjoy it."

He turned the book from front cover to back. "Too thick."

"It'll go fast, once you get into it," she promised.

"Are there a lot of big words?"

"Some. Just ask me, if you don't understand any."

It took him almost two months, but he finished the book.

Thus began Lorne's new appreciation of the artistic and cultural life. There were many more books to be read. Together, he and Aunt Rose visited city museums, went to the movies, and saw Broadway plays. Whenever he went to the theater, he left feeling as if he were one of the characters he had just seen.

Outside the convenience store, Lorne watched the morning sun wash the mountains. An older man sat down next to him. Lorne offered some nachos, which the man politely declined. Then jabbing his long chin toward the mountain range, the old-timer said, "Somethin', isn't is?"

"Sure is," Lorne replied, welcoming the company.

"And you know what?" the man continued. "As beautiful as the mountains are, they make me sad. They were there long before I came along, and they'll be there long after I'm gone."

"Makes you think about how fleeting life is," Lorne added.

"Well, the mountains are very special to me."

"Me, too," said Lorne. He could have sat there all day, but he realized he had many more miles to go. He got up, finished his coffee, and threw the container in a nearby barrel. A bottle of water in hand for the journey ahead, he said, "See you, partner. Nice meeting you," and walked back to the car.

Brushing himself off, Lorne reached into his jeans pocket for his car keys and two treasured remnants of the past—a gold-plated key and a baby sock. They weren't there.

He searched all his pockets. "Damn!" Back in the Camry, Lorne continued to look for the sock and key, but without success. Hiding his irritation, he picked up his cell phone and dialed the rental office that handled the home where he lived. He was brief and to the point when the manager answered.

"Hello, Mr. Kelsey, Peter Fox here. Hate to give you such short notice, but I had to move out in a hurry, emergency in the family. I left the keys to the house on the kitchen table. I think you'll find everything in order. I'm paid up until the end of the month, so we're all square, and you can keep whatever is left over. I've left a few pieces of furniture. Maybe you can use them."

"Well, that's very generous of you, Mr. Fox. Thank you very much."

"Don't mention it. Oh, one more thing," said Lorne as nonchalantly as possible. "I'm missing a couple of small items, including a gold-plated key and a baby sock, just stuff that has sentimental value to me." He laughed nervously, then continued,

"If you find anything like that, just hold onto them. I'll call and tell you where to send them."

"Sure thing, Mr. Fox. No problem."

"Great, Mr. Kelsey." That settled, Lorne put his head back against the headrest and closed his road-weary eyes. Moments later, he woke up with a start, laughing at how quickly he had fallen asleep. He turned on the engine and continued his journey. As he drove, he thought about what the old-timer said. Once again, the memory of an earlier time flooded his brain ...

By the age of sixteen, Lorne was so interested in acting he began auditioning for roles in the theater. He landed none, mainly because of his age and lack of experience. Then an off-Broadway director took a chance and picked him to play a small but edgy role in a new drama. The play flopped, but he received a nice review. Even then, he loved playing character parts.

It was around this time that he met Frances Hart. She was a pretty girl his age, with stunning green eyes and glistening black hair. Lorne had seen her around the neighborhood, but he never spoke with her. She was quiet and seemed a bit shy.

Then one day, outside the library, he made a point to introduce himself.

"Oh, hi, I'm Lorne Bennett. My friends call me Lorney."

"Hi, I know who you know," she said, almost in a whisper. "You're the actor."

"Well, not yet," he replied. "I'm working on it."

She nodded, smiled and introduced herself. She had a warm, beautiful smile. Lorne liked her right away. He discreetly searched his pockets for change. He had some. "Want to grab a soda or something?" he offered.

"Can't, thanks. Got to do some homework," she replied, gesturing toward the library.

"Me, too," he lied, hoping she wouldn't notice that he left his school books home.

For the next hour, they sat in the library, hardly saying a word to each other. She was going over notes for a history exam; he was reading magazines. When they were finished, they left together and started going their separate ways. Then, Lorne stopped, turned, and ran back to her.

"Mind if I walk you home?" he said.

Frances smiled. "No."

Over the next several weeks, they got to know each other pretty well. Lorne discovered that Frances was the daughter of a single mom. Beneath her shyness was a sincere, intelligent person with strong, heartfelt feelings she was willing to share, once she got to know you. She was just a nice person, he concluded.

Before long, it became obvious to the whole neighborhood that they were a twosome, while Lorne and Frances found themselves in an intense, all-consuming relationship. Then one night when her mother was working, they discovered each other in a new and beautiful way. It was the first of several such deep, sensual encounters.

The young couple became inseparable Then one day in June, Lorne was offered a good part in a Eugene O'Neill play on Cape Cod. Overjoyed, he accepted. But Frances, who was looking forward to a long, glorious summer with him, was devastated. They argued, briefly, but Lorne stuck to his decision and went to the Cape. He did well, winning rave reviews for an exciting performance.

When he returned home, his relationship with Frances seemed to change. They tried to reignite the flame, but what Lorne wanted most was to pursue a career as an actor. He broke up with Frances. Simple as that. But it was the saddest and most difficult decision he had ever made. Frances, after all, was his first real love. What else could he have done? Things were starting to move so fast in his direction, and life was too short.

13

When Lorne arrived in Las Vegas, he decided to play it safe rather than fight the traffic and the crowds for a room in one of the glitzier hotels on the Strip. Wearing tinted glasses he didn't need and a fake moustache trimmed inconspicuously under a nose lightly made up to soften its sharp contours, he checked into a motel in the older part of the town. Exhausted from the long ride, he headed straight for his room, where he stayed for the next two days, with occasional forays into the surrounding area for something to eat.

By the third day, he felt comfortable enough to chat with the motel's staff, including Maria, the housekeeper. She was a Mexican immigrant with a bright, toothy smile who lived in an apartment in the Valley with her husband and three small children. Like so many others, she came to Las Vegas to make enough money so that she and Edgar, her husband, could buy their own home. What Lorne liked about her was that she never asked him questions, and she always wished him "a very nice day, Mr. Fox."

Carmella, at the front desk, was not as sociable, but after her initial distrust wore off—and Lorne felt that this distrust was directed at anyone who walked into the lobby for the first time—she could be quite friendly and talkative. In her late forties, she was a robust woman with a cherubic face. A Long Islander by birth, Carmella came to Vegas thirty years earlier with her single mom, Lorne discovered. Being from the East himself, he liked talking with her and appreciated her New York sense of humor when she felt kindly enough to share it. Besides, she saved a *USA Today* and an apple every day for him. And she, too, didn't ask a lot of questions.

Of all the people Lorne met at the hotel, Carl Kurtz was the most forlorn-looking. When he first saw him, Lorne had the impression that the bell-hop had lost his best friend and precious possessions all in one day, which, as it turned out, was not that far from the truth.

In his mid-sixties, Carl was a hard worker who served as a handyman, parking attendant, and luggage carrier. He had been employed at the motel for almost twenty-five years. His loyalty, Lorne later learned, had endeared him to the family owners and allowed him privileges other employees didn't have, including a two-room flat in the basement. Though taciturn, he was friendly enough, with a pleasant, weathered face that commanded attention, and he was quick to help the customer. That's how Lorne met him.

"Is there anywhere I can access a computer?" Lorne asked him one day.

"Oh, so sorry. We don't have any," Carl explained in a slight German accent. "As you can see, we are a fine, small motel with none of the distractions those big, fancy places on the Strip offer." Lorne thought he saw a smug smile cross Carl's face.

"How about an Internet service store?"

Carl looked a bit puzzled.

"You know, a place where the public can go in and rent the use of a computer for an hour or two."

"Oh, yes, I think I saw one on Commerce Street ... but come with me."

Carl led him to the elevator and pressed the "LL" button. Lorne had always wanted to know what was on the lower level.

When he entered Carl's apartment, Lorne saw a place crammed with furniture, boxes, and other odds and ends, but somehow everything was neatly arranged. Carl led him to a desk in the corner and flicked on the floor lamp.

"Here, use mine, Mister ..."

"Fox, Peter Fox. Thanks."

Next to the desk was a wall of photographs, which Lorne surveyed quickly. One picture in particular caught his attention. It showed a young Carl and a beautiful, blonde-haired woman standing on each side of a smallish, dappled horse. In the saddle was a pretty young girl in riding gear, a proud smile on her face.

"Your family?" Lorne inquired.

"Yes," said Carl. "That's Frieda, my wife ... and that's my daughter, Ilse." He cleared his throat. "They're both gone, killed in a train crash in Montana twenty-six years ago. Do you have family, Mr. Fox?"

"Yes."

"Hold them close. Treasure them. They are very precious," said Carl, heading toward the front door. "Please make yourself comfortable," he added. "I have some work to do. Just close the front door when you leave."

It didn't take Lorne long to find what he was looking for— the home page of the *Mesa Morning Record.* Turning to its archive of news stories, he searched the lineup until he found it: "Runaway Car Near Apache Junction." He read the article. Typical community news.

The story was accompanied by a photo of a crowd of people peering at a Camry dangling on the edge of a swimming pool. In the foreground were two police officers talking to a man Lorne recognized as himself. Under the photo was the credit line: "Photo by Billy Volpe." There were no other pictures with the story. Lorne jotted down the photographer's name. As he got up and walked to the door, he looked at the photograph of Carl's family again and thought about what he had said.

Somehow, memories of Aurora, and the first time he met her, came to mind ...

She was flat on her butt in the middle of the Rockefeller Center ice skating rink. He was making a movie, kissing the leading lady in the final scene, and she was an extra. "Cut!" the director shouted.

Lorne skated over and helped Aurora to her feet. She was tall and extraordinarily beautiful with hazel eyes and dark hair tied in a ponytail away from her smooth, flawless face. "God, you could be a model," he said when he saw her up close.

"I am," she said.

"What are you doing here?" he asked.

"I want to be in the movies," she told him.

"Good reason. Can you skate?"

"No, not really, but a gal's got to start somewhere."

Lorne was struck by her directness and simplicity as well as her beauty. "Maybe I can help you."

"Oh, one of those," she shot back. "Sorry, I don't do couches."

"Neither do I," said Lorne. "What's your name?"

"If you really want to know, it's Helen Ames, but everyone calls me Aurora."

"Nice to meet you. My name's Lorne Bennett."

"I know. I heard all about you."

"Can't believe everything you read."

"You know what they say, Where there's smoke ..."

It wasn't easy tracking her down the next day, but he finally found her phone number and called her. He was surprised when a man with a deep, mellow voice answered.

"Thanks, dad," said Aurora, when she picked up the phone.

"Oh, that was your father," said Lorne, a bit relieved.

"Who did you think it was?" she said playfully. "Here's how it goes: I live with my dad, he lives with my mom and me, and we all live together with my sister Sally here in New Jersey."

"Sounds like one happy family."

"Well, yes and no," she said. "Would you like to meet them?"

Once again Lorne was struck by her directness. "Sure."

They set a date before launching into small talk on a smattering of topics, including the weather (a snowstorm was brewing), the movies, and the people they knew. When he hung up, Lorne sat quietly, reliving the conversation. Usually confident by the way he handled himself, he wondered. *Did I say the right things?*

Lorne was welcomed warmly when he arrived at the Ames' home two days later. From all appearances, Eve and Jesse Ames and their two daughters seemed to be a close, loving family. Aurora's natural friendliness and sense of humor made him feel at home, and her mother was just as lively and gregarious. Sally, like her father, seemed more serious, but she relaxed later.

Dinner was delicious, topped by a towering homemade chocolate layer cake. Lorne was slightly embarrassed but delighted, and he became emotional when Aurora served the cake with a single lit candle on top.

"How did you know I'll be twenty-one next week?" he laughed.

"I did my homework," she replied.

"What else did you discover?"

"I don't have enough time to tell you, but if you're twenty-one, I'm eighteen."

Toward the end of a long, relaxing day, Lorne sat with Aurora on the porch looking out the window. The snow was beginning to fall.

"You going to be alright going home in that?" asked Aurora.

"Sure, no problem," he replied.

"You're welcome to stay."

"Thanks, but I like driving in the snow. It slows everything down, and I can see the world around me for a change."

They sat quietly watching the landscape turn white. Lorne finally broke the silence. "In the old days, they would have said, 'Are you spoken for?' "

"If you mean 'Am I seeing anyone?' the answer is No. Not now," she replied. "There was a guy, a nice guy, and we were pretty serious at one time, but that's over now. I just wasn't ready to settle down. Know what I mean?"

"Yes, I do."

The light was fading fast. Lorne got up, and Aurora rose with him. "I'd better be going," he announced. They stood awkwardly looking into each other's eyes. Then she reached over and held his hands. "Call me," she said. He smiled, welcoming her suggestion. They embraced and kissed. Feeling her soft, warm body close to him, he didn't want to go.

"You're so beautiful you must have drove that guy crazy," he whispered. "I'll call when I get home."

After three months, they decided to share a loft in the city while they continued to pursue separate careers. Lorne kept exploring scripts in search of exciting new characters and flying back and forth from coast to coast. When he found a role he liked, he arranged it so they were living together wherever they were shooting.

With Lorne's intercession, Aurora managed to land a couple of small parts. Her dazzling beauty overshadowed her acting, and she gradually cast aside her movie ambitions while continuing to pursue occasional modeling jobs and traveling extensively with Lorne.

Two years after they met, they were married. The image of the two of them coming out of that small church in New Jersey caught the public's imagination all over the world. Glowing with love and joy, they were considered the darlings of the media, and fans felt they were the couple "most likely to live happily ever after." Aurora told Lorne that she would have preferred that they be called "the couple most likely to have a family and to live happily ever after."

From his small Las Vegas hotel, Lorne could feel the excitement of the city around him, but he would have none of it this time. In the past, Vegas had been his escape from the intense pressures of Hollywood life. It was a place where he could almost relax and have some fun with his West Coast buddies, most of whom were originally from the East. But the harsh glare of the city could only expose him now, so he intended to stay as close as possible to his inconspicuous residence.

Aurora would have liked that, he thought. Las Vegas was not her favorite town. She saw it as a powerful attraction that pulled them apart and threatened their marriage, and she'd tell him so. She preferred that they stay home whenever they weren't working, spending some quiet and playful time together and working on building a family.

Lorne tried to respect her feelings, but he couldn't give up the nightlife entirely. Even when they moved into an elegant apartment in a quiet, trendy part of New York City, he would steal away to visit his old friends from the neighborhood, sometimes returning the following day. As those nighttime excursions continued, Aurora grew angrier.

Over time, the arguments between them became more heated, and their verbal clashes erupted in public, reaching a peak of fury and frustration in the weeks after Laura was born.

Those should have been the happiest days for the couple, but they weren't. The happiness they felt as they walked down the aisle of that small church in New Jersey seemed so far away.

14

Lorne Bennett decided to make the call. He just had to take the risk in order to protect himself from further exposure in the media and a reinvigorated manhunt by the police and FBI. He had found Billy Volpe's listed phone number easily enough. The more difficult part was waiting for someone to pick up the phone. One ring, two rings, three, four ...

A girl finally answered, a bit breathlessly.

"Oh hi, this is Peter Fox," he said. "Who's this?"

"Call me Alex. Everyone does."

Lorne liked her friendliness. "May I speak to Mr. Volpe, Alex?"

"Dad's not here. He's in Phoenix on a story. May I help you?"

He hesitated, then decided to plunge ahead. "It's about some pictures your father took of a car accident a few days ago."

"Excuse me."

In the background, a TV weather woman was going on about an unexpected rainstorm in Las Vegas. Lorne turned down the volume. "Sorry," he continued. "It's about some photographs your father took for the *Mesa Morning Record*. About a Camry that accidentally went rolling down the hill and into a construction area."

"Oh, you mean the runaway car," said Alex. She seemed to be moving things around as she talked.

"Yes. I'd like to buy all rights to them." Then he laughed nervously, as he was prone to do when he was about to say something that covered up his real intent. "No big deal. I want to put together an album. I want to show some friends back East what I'm up to in my retirement out here in the bad old West. I'm sure they'll get a kick out of it."

"I suppose so, especially since no one got hurt."

"Yes, that's true. Please let your dad know I'll call him back later with a box number."

"Sure, Mr. Fox. I'll tell him."

Ten minutes after she hung up the phone, Billy Volpe—hot, tired, and famished—pulled into the driveway. When he opened the front door, Alex grabbed him by the arm and pulled him into the living room.

"Guess who was on the phone trying to reach you a few minutes ago."

" 'Sixty Minutes'?"

"No. Better. Peter Fox."

"NO!"

"YES! He wants to buy all rights to the photos you took of the accident."

"I bet he does."

"Says he'll call you later with a box number."

"How did he sound? Nervous? Friendly? Scared?" he wanted to know.

"All of those things."

"I wish I knew where he was," said Billy.

"Thank you, caller ID and TV weather lady. He's in Las Vegas," she disclosed.

Billy swept her up and kissed her on the cheek. "What's for dinner?"

"Turkey meatballs. Trudi gave me a recipe."

"I guess this is my lucky day."

Later that day, Lorne was ready to take Carl Kurtz out to dinner. It was the only decent thing to do. After all, how many people allow a stranger to come into their home, then walk out, and let the stranger work on their computer? Lorne had felt an immediate kinship when he first met Carl. And now, as he was about to dine with the bell-hop, he felt the emergence of a friendship and trust based on the commonality of a painful past. Lorne brushed his hair one more time and put on a pale blue blazer. He was ready to go.

But first he would call Billy Volpe, as promised. When Billy answered the phone, Lorne explained how anxious he was to buy the photos of the accident and offered him his box number. He also told Billy that he'd be willing to pay "whatever you want— within reason, of course."

After a slight pause, Billy said, "Well, here's the thing, Mr. Fox. I'm going to Las Vegas tomorrow morning. Instead of mailing you the pictures, I'd be happy to drop them off to you if you're going to be in the area."

Lorne thought about that for a few seconds. "Why not?" he said finally. "If it's not too much for you ..."

"No problem."

They agreed to meet the following afternoon by the lion statue in the lobby of the MGM Grand.

"Sounds good," said Billy. "I'll be with a precocious twelve-year-old."

"Do you mean Alex?" asked Lorne

"Yes."

"Great, see you both tomorrow."

Heading down to the lobby, Lorne, ever the cautious one, wondered whether he was starting to let his guard down too much. *I'm going out with the bell-hop tonight, and tomorrow I have a date with the Volpes. Am I pushing the envelope?*

He hardly recognized Carl when he got off the elevator. Out of uniform, the bell-hop looked like a different person. Dressed in a tan suit, which looked a bit too tight on him, Carl waved when he saw Lorne coming toward him.

"I took the liberty of pulling your car out front," he said, shoving the collar of his white shirt under his lapel.

"Thanks, Carl. I'm sure you know the way."

"Of course, Mr. Fox."

"Peter, please."

"Okay, tonight it is Peter."

The restaurant was a small, quiet place offering an international cuisine. A bartender in long shirt sleeves was serving drinks to two customers seated on stools at a curved bar in the front of the restaurant. Seven or eight tables were sprinkled neatly and strategically in a narrow dining area that led to swinging doors to the kitchen. Carl was instantly recognized, which surprised Lorne, and the two were led to their table.

"Nice to be known," Carl commented, a sly smile on his face.

"Sometimes ... I suppose," said Lorne.

Enjoying a leisurely dinner of Scandinavian dishes pleasantly interrupted by sips of a fine California pinot noir, they chatted about everything but themselves. The weather, always a good ice breaker. The changing face of Vegas. The old motel where they were staying. Its history. The history of its owners. Their conversation had the reserved, professional tone of a public radio interview. Most of the time, Lorne was the interviewer, but sometimes it was difficult to tell who was interviewer and who was guest.

Finally, sometime between the entree and the coffee, Carl steered the conversation into less charted waters. "You know, Peter, Las Vegas has been very good to me. After my wife and daughter died, I left Montana and came to Las Vegas, not knowing a soul but determined to make a new life for myself. I got a job at the motel and threw myself into my work. I guess the people there liked what they saw, and they kept expanding my responsibilities and opportunities. I can't thank them enough for giving me a lift when I needed it. Do you know what I mean?"

Lorne nodded.

"Now, Peter, tell me a little about yourself."

It was as if he unexpectedly came face to face with the last person he ever wanted to see. Lorne froze. Then, not knowing how to answer Carl's question, he reached for the bottle of wine and knocked over a glass of water. A waiter rushed over and mopped up the table. Lorne apologized, but, applying his training as an actor, he kept his composure.

"I guess you just can't bring some people to nice places," Lorne said with a straight face.

Carl smiled patiently.

Sweat beaded up on Lorne's forehead. "Well, the short version is, like you, I'm a widower. I have a daughter who's twenty-two and living in New York City. I'm originally from New York myself, but I've been living in the Southwest for the past five years."

"Are you retired?"

"Yes, but I don't feel like it. I travel a lot, I read everything I get my hands on, and I've been doing some research on the history of the movies. It's sort of a hobby. Maybe I'll write a book someday."

"You are too young to be retired."

Lorne smiled appreciatively.

"What about your daughter?" Carl asked. "Do you see her often?"

"She's working as a copywriter at an advertising agency." Lorne paused, an overwhelming sadness in his eyes. "No, I don't see her much. We can't seem to connect," he said absently.

Perhaps he could change the subject. "Coffee?" Lorne asked. Carl nodded. Lorne ordered for both of them, and just as quickly the coffee was served.

Carl took a sip of his and brushed off a crumb from the table. "We have a lot in common, you and I," he continued. "But, if you don't mind my saying so, maybe you ought to stop doing whatever you're doing and take the time to see your daughter. What is her name?"

"Laura," said Lorne, as an elderly man in a checkered blazer headed toward their table. Did someone else recognize him?

"Oh, so nice to see you again, Carl," said the stranger. They shook hands. Carl turned toward Lorne. "Meet my friend, Peter Fox."

Later, when they returned to the motel, Carl thanked Lorne

for "an evening I will always remember," adding, "If you ever need anything, anything, just let me know."

"It was wonderful," said Lorne.

Then Carl asked him if he would mind coming to his room for a minute. "I want to show you something." Lorne agreed.

In the apartment, Carl found what he was looking for in a large chest: an album bulging with photographs, illustrations, and other oddities. He flicked on the floor lamp and placed the album on a table. "You said you were researching the history of the movies. This is something I've been working on for some time. I'm quite a movie fan. Here, take a look. May I get you a drink?"

"Water would be fine," said Lorne.

As Carl walked away, Lorne started flipping through the pages. He recognized many faces from his Hollywood days. Finally, there they were—"The West Side Kid", the master of disguises, and his wife Aurora. Lorne moved quickly past that photo and through the rest of the album. Thankfully, he couldn't find any other photos of himself.

"This is quite an album," he said when Carl returned.

"Yes, isn't it?" said Carl, handing him a glass of water. "I look through it all the time. I remember a lot of those people. What interests me the most is not so much what they did in the movies, but the kind of things they did in real life."

Lorne cleared his throat. "As I said, it's quite a collection. I'd like to borrow it sometime."

"Sure, anytime."

Lorne took another sip. "I better be going. It's been a long day."

They shook hands again. "Remember what I said, Peter. If you ever need anything ..."

15

The flight from Phoenix to Las Vegas the next morning promised to be a short, pleasant trip. Billy looked over at Alex. Not a very seasoned flyer, she was clinging to the armrests for dear life, her eyes responding to every movement within the cabin.

"You can let go now," said Billy. "We're airborne."

Alex shook her head.

"Look at that gorgeous sky."

She quickly turned to the window and back. "Very nice."

"Why don't you read or listen to some music?" he suggested.

"No, I'd just like to sit here quietly and meditate, if you don't mind."

"I don't mind, Alex. But maybe you should meditate on the fact that the people flying this plane know what they're doing."

"You don't know that for sure, dad," she said, closing her eyes after the aircraft banked to the left.

"Suit yourself. While you're choking those armrests, I'll just have some coffee and try to relax. Can't wait to get there." He was excited, but not for the usual reasons people are when they visit Vegas. He was anxious to meet Lorne Bennett, the movie star suspected of killing his wife, or, as he kept reminding himself,

Peter Fox, the man with the runaway car. Was this the pot of gold at the end of the rainbow for the reporter?

When they arrived at the MGM Grand, they checked in and rolled their bags straight up to their room. Alex flopped on one of the beds.

"Do you think he really did it?" she wondered out loud.

"Did what?" asked Billy, as he started trimming his beard in the mirror.

"Murder his wife."

"Well, I don't know," he theorized, "but there's some strong circumstantial evidence that points to him. From what we've read, they were having big marital difficulties. They were seen fighting in public several times. Apparently, he liked his good times with his friends; she wanted him to spend more time at home. He had an alibi but it was weak. He said he was out drinking with his West Side friends, but they couldn't say for sure where he was at the time of the killing. Plus, nothing was stolen or disturbed at the apartment where she was killed, and his gun was missing.

"Here's the clincher as far as I'm concerned," he continued. "Why would anyone run away if he didn't have anything to do with the crime? And what kind of a guy would up and leave his four-month-old daughter with his sister-in-law?" Recalling that Trudi had left Alex at an early age, he wished he had not said that.

Alex answered the question anyway. "Someone who was very, very frightened."

"Maybe."

"Dad, are we crazy?" she went on. "I mean, if he did it, shouldn't he be considered dangerous? What are we doing meeting him? Shouldn't we be calling the police or the FBI or someone?"

Billy stopped trimming his beard and sat down on the opposite bed. "I know this may sound selfish, Alex, but this could be the biggest break I ever had," he began. "You know how long, and how often, I've talked about getting the big story. This is it. It has all the elements: A major Hollywood actor, under suspicion of murdering his beautiful wife, on the run for twenty-two years. And we're going to meet with him today. Wherever you turn, there are questions. How did he manage to get away? Where did he go? Did anyone help him along the way?"

"And the big question," she added. "Did he kill his wife?"

"Yeah, that's the big one. Don't worry, Alex. If I think we're in any danger, I won't hesitate to call in the cavalry." He started trimming his moustache now. "What about you, Alex? Do you think he did it?"

"I'll tell you after I see him and talk with him. They say guilt or innocence is in the facial expressions, especially the eyes and the mouth."

"Then, let's get a good look at him."

"And, as long as we're here, let's not forget the MGM lions, dad. I'd really like to see them."

There was a knock on the door. They both jumped up. When Billy opened the door, no one was there. He looked down the hallway. A little boy, probably four or five, was running down the corridor and laughing, a man—probably his father—in close pursuit.

At the appointed hour, Lorne immediately spotted Billy when he came into the lobby. He walked up to him. "Nice seeing you again," said Lorne, extending his hand in greeting. "You mind if I call you Billy?"

Billy didn't seem to recognize the tall, handsome man in front of him. Then the light went on. "No, Billy's fine," he said, breaking out into a smile. "Tell you the truth I didn't know who you were at first, Mr. Fox."

"It's Peter. It was pretty dark and hectic the night we met."

"You look different to me," Billy observed. "Maybe it's the moustache and the glasses."

"They're both new."

"That explains it. Come, meet my daughter."

As they walked around to the other side, Alex had her feet folded under her on the marble bench surrounding the majestic statue. She jumped up when she saw her father and the stranger.

Her excitement seemed warm and welcoming. Lorne's face lit up.

"Hi, Alex. I'm so glad to meet you," he beamed, extending his hand to her.

"My father's family always kiss when they say hello and good-bye," she said.

"I like that custom," said the tall man. He bent over and kissed the girl on the cheek. Billy joined the moment; he kissed his daughter on the other cheek.

Alex laughed. "Have you seen the lions yet?" she asked.

"Actually, no," Lorne replied.

"What do you say, dad?"

"Why not?" Billy responded.

"I know exactly where they are," said Alex, reaching out to hold Lorne's hand.

Lorne wanted to pull away at first. It had been a long time since he had held anyone's hand. But then, in the wretched loneliness he lately had felt, he often wondered what it would be like to be with his daughter, listen to her, laugh with her, simply hold her hand. Alex's hand was warm and friendly. He liked the feeling.

For the next two hours, they visited the lions' exhibit and toured the hotel, walking at a leisurely pace, casually commenting on something they saw, obviously enjoying each other's company. Lorne had not been as relaxed since he was in Bali where he spent many hours sitting on the beach and gazing out at the sea. He thought of it as his "quality time with the ocean," a time of renewal, when he would draw strength and encouragement from the sea.

They decided to take a walk across the street to the New York, New York casino hotel.

"It brings back memories," said Billy as they reached the entrance to the place.

"It looks like the real thing, only smaller," Lorne laughed.

"I was born in the Bronx," Billy noted.

"Oh, oh, here it comes," said Alex.

"Well, I was. I was a little kid, but I remember a lot, and then I visited the city years later." Billy paused, then added, "Did you live in the city, Peter?"

"Oh, yes, a long time ago. East Side, West Side, all around the town. Like they say, it's a wonderful town."

"Do you miss it?" asked Alex.

Lorne paused, then said, "Yes, I do, But I make my home under the western sky now." Maybe he had said enough. "Hey, anyone else hungry?" he quickly added. "I don't know about you, but just watching those lions eat made me hungry."

"Yeah, I know what you mean," Billy chuckled.

"Yuk!" said Alex. "I think you've both seen too many nature TV shows."

They found a restaurant, and Lorne arranged for the three of them to sit in a corner booth, away from—but not totally out of sight of—the main body of the restaurant. He took off his sunglasses and laid them on the table. Then he pulled out a book of matches and lit a candle that served as a centerpiece.

Drinks were ordered all around—a Chablis for Billy, a large chocolate milk for Alex, and an Amstel Light and Pepsi for Lorne. After the previous evening's Scandinavian fare, Lorne ordered a hamburger special. Billy went for the fish and chips. Alex opted for a chicken salad.

Old habits never die easily. Once in a while, Lorne stole a glance around the room for any suspicious characters, but, by and large, he had not felt this relaxed in ages. As they ate, he enjoyed hearing Alex tell stories about her life growing up in Arizona, her friends and school, and her plans for the future.

"I haven't made up my mind, really," she said. "I'm torn between being a mystery writer, preferably nonfiction, and a CIA spy. And, oh, there's one other possibility."

"What's that?" Lorne inquired.

"Cactus grower."

"What would the Southwest be without cactus plants?" she noted. "You wouldn't believe how many different forms of cactus are out here."

"Isn't that amazing?" said Lorne.

"And with so many people moving into the area and the droughts and the pollution, somebody has to take care of those poor plants," she added.

"That's a very noble ambition, Alex," Lorne concluded.

There was a thoughtful silence.

"Look, before I forget, I have your pictures, Peter," said Billy, yanking everyone back to reality. "I made copies of all of them, and I've included the flash memory card as well." He handed him an envelope. "They're all yours now."

"Oh, thank you very much. Do I own the rights?"

"Well, I have a set in my computer, but I don't plan to do anything with them."

Lorne was silent for a moment. "How much do I owe you?"

"Not a penny. I think you paid enough with the accident."

"Oh, come on, I insist ..."

"Please, it's my pleasure. I hope your friends and relatives back East enjoy them."

"Thanks." Lorne looked across the room again. Tucked in the corner was a booth of four people—an older couple and two girls around six or seven years of age. Probably the grandparents and their grandchildren on vacation, Lorne conjectured. The man, who was wearing a Hawaiian shirt, was leaning his head on his elbow and looking directly at him. Lorne briefly exchanged glances with him, then turned away.

A slow heat rose to the back of his neck. *Was that Bud Turner, the detective who had handled my wife's case for so many years?* Turner was the one who had interviewed him after Aurora was found dead. *What is he doing here?* Then, Lorne remembered that Turner had recently retired and a new man was placed in charge of the case, according to his pals back East.

His instincts were to get up and beat it out of there as fast as he could, but that would only draw attention. Donning his glasses, he picked up a napkin and dabbed the sweat from his forehead. *Play it cool! Don't overreact!*

Lorne glanced at his watch. "Oh, my goodness, it's almost four o'clock. I think I'd better be going. Where did the time go?" He looked at Billy and Alex. "I hope you don't mind ... I had a great time." Then, catching the eye of a passing waiter, he said, "Check, please." The waiter nodded and sped off to the register.

"Are you okay?" asked Billy.

"I'm fine," he replied, forcing a smile. "I just remembered an appointment and a few other things I have to do. Please excuse me. It was fun."

"Oh, that's alright, Mr. Fox," said Alex. "Maybe, if you have time later, we can go for a walk on the Strip."

"Oh, I really can't. I'd love to, another time," said Lorne. When the waiter came back with the check, he glanced at it and peeled off some twenties. Then he rose from the table and glanced once more at the man across the room. The man was whispering something in the woman's ear, while the two girls were giggling.

"Can I give you a lift to wherever you're going?" Billy offered. "I rented a car at the airport. We're driving back home."

"No, thanks, Billy. I'll just hop a cab."

"Well, so long, Mr. Fox," said Alex. She slid out of the booth and stood up. This time, *she* kissed *him* on the cheek.

"Thanks, Alex, I needed that. Good-bye, Billy. I had a great time." Alex looked like she wanted him to stay. But just like that, he was gone.

Billy and Alex were about to leave the restaurant when the man in the Hawaiian shirt crossed the room and came up to them.

"Excuse me," he said. "The man who was sitting with you over there, is he a friend or a relative?"

"Just a casual acquaintance," Billy replied. "Why?"

"He looks like somebody I knew in New York. Would you mind telling me his name?"

"Why? Is there a problem?" Billy asked.

"Oh, no, not really."

"In that case," said Billy, "his name is Peter Fox."

"No, no, I don't think that's the same guy."

"And what is your name?" Alex asked in a voice flowing with innocence.

He looked down and smiled. "Bud Turner." Then, turning to

Billy, Turner asked, "Do you know where Mr. Fox is staying in Las Vegas?"

"No, I'm sorry. Like I said, he was just a casual acquaintance," Billy replied. "Your first time in Vegas?"

"Yes, as a matter of fact," said the man. "I just retired. Me and the wife are here with the grandkids."

"Hope you're having a great time," said Alex.

As they walked away, Billy turned to Alex. "Now I know why our friend was in such a hurry. He must have known that guy." Billy could feel the big story slipping away, but he didn't care. "I wish I knew where he was staying," he said. "I'd like to let him know someone was asking for him. I kind of feel sorry for him."

"So do I." She reached into her purse and pulled out the book of matches Lorne had used to light the candle on the table. It carried the name of a motel in the older part of town. "Will this help?"

16

LORNE KNEW HE HAD TO ACT QUICKLY. BACK
at the hotel, he checked out and bade Carmella a warm good-
bye. He hurried up to his room and threw his clothes and some
other personal belongings into two large bags and squeezed some
essentials—some papers, medications, a few toiletries, and his
disguise kit—into a carry-on. Then, drawing a deep breath, he
called for the bell-hop.

Lorne planted a smile on his face as he opened the door.
"That's what I like about small motels," he said, "when you call for
a bell-hop, you know who's coming."

Carl Kurtz looked more forlorn than usual when he saw
the bags lined up on the floor. "Don't tell me you are leaving! Is
everything alright?"

"A personal emergency," Lorne explained. "I had planned to
stay a few more days, but I have to leave now."

"Oh, I am so sorry to hear that," said Carl. "I was hoping to
take *you* out to dinner this time."

"Another time," said Lorne. He closed the door behind Carl.
"Did you really mean what you said last night? About letting you
know if I ever needed anything?"

"Absolutely."

"Well, I need to leave in a hurry, and where I'm headed is pretty far from here, and I don't know when I'll be back here."

"Yes?"

"Would you mind taking ownership of my car?"

"Oh my goodness! I would be happy to, if you wish."

"It's a pretty decent car and served me well, and you might want to have it checked out, but I really can't take it with me where I'm going."

"I understand."

Lorne reached for an envelope on an end table and handed it to Carl. "The ownership papers and extra keys are in that envelope. They're yours to do with however you see fit. Maybe you'd like to take a trip back to Montana."

"Thank you. You are too kind." Carl's eyes were glistening now. "Now, let me help you with your bags, Mr. Fox."

Billy Volpe was pulling into the motel's parking lot when he spotted Lorne. "There's our man," he whispered. From a safe distance, he and Alex took notice as Lorne shook hands with the bell-hop and jumped into a taxi. "Let's go, dad." Billy followed the cab out of the lot and onto the roadway. It wasn't long before they realized they were headed for the airport.

When they saw Lorne exit the cab and enter the United terminal, they jumped out of the car and followed him. There was no more time to waste. There was no doubt in Billy's mind that the police would be scouring the airport for Peter Fox now. But by the time they got into the terminal, Lorne had already checked his two large bags and headed to the gate for his flight to Hawaii.

"There he is, dad, there he is," said Alex under her breath. "Oh, my God! Turn around, quick, or he'll see us, dad."

"Isn't that the whole idea, Alex? Come on, let's go talk to him."

Lorne paled when he saw them walking toward him. "What are you two doing here?" he murmured, placing his carry-on on the floor.

"We've come to warn you," said Billy.

"About what?" Lorne asked.

"After you left the restaurant, a man came up to us," Billy explained. "He said he thought he knew you in New York. His name was Bud Turner."

Lorne's hands clenched down into fists.

"I'm not sure I did the right thing," Billy continued. "He asked your name, and I told him Peter Fox."

"How did you know where I was?" Lorne inquired.

"We followed you from the motel," Alex replied.

"And how did you know where I was staying?"

"It was on the matchbook you left on the table," Alex explained.

Lorne shook his head in disbelief. He glanced at the clock on the wall. Then turning to Billy and Alex, he said. "Look, my plane leaves soon. I appreciate your coming all the way out here to see me, but you should go now."

"All we want to do is help you," said Billy. He hesitated, then added, "Don't you think it's time you stopped running, Mr. Bennett?"

Lorne was startled. Realizing his secret was shared by two more people—and only God knew how many more. "If you want to help me," Lorne said, "you'll walk away, forget you saw me, and let me board my plane."

"Let's go, dad," said Alex. "Good-bye, Mr. Bennett. It was very nice meeting you. I wish we could have spent more time together."

"Take care," Billy added.

Lorne watched them slowly make their way out of the terminal. *Good people, nice people. They took a chance coming here. How sweet it was holding Alex's warm, friendly hand this afternoon! I could have done the same thing with my Laura. Billy meant well. After twenty-two years, who wouldn't want to stop running? Hell, I've been running all my life!*

As he walked toward his gate, Lorne could hear the first boarding instructions. Two men in suits gave him a suspicious look as they brushed past him and headed for the front of the terminal. Lorne knew what he had to do now. There was no way he was going to board, or even attempt to board, that plane. They would be waiting to pick up Peter Fox.

It was a no-brainer. He would need a new destination and a new identity. He went into the nearest men's room, put on sunglasses and a sweatshirt and added a little makeup to change his appearance. When he came out, the last call for the United flight to Hawaii was being announced. Lorne melded in with a group of passengers who had just arrived and headed for the baggage pickup area and the exits. As he walked into the desert heat, a gentle breeze embraced him and encouraged him to keep on going. There were two things he needed now: new clothes and new luggage.

PART 4

THE HOUND OF HELL

17

It was Monday, and Laura Bennett had just arrived in the lobby of the building where she worked. She was waiting to board the elevator when she felt a tap on her shoulder. It was Anita Tedesco, a disapproving look on her face.

"What's going on?" asked Anita, pulling Laura away from the elevator crowd.

"Nothing. I'm fine, really," Laura replied.

"You look like a mummy on a bad hair day," said Anita, speaking in a whisper. "Come on, let me fix your hair."

"What's wrong with my hair?"

"It's as flat as my ass. Come on. I was a hairdresser in my past life."

In a ladies room off the lobby, Anita pulled, fluffed, and brushed Laura's hair back to life. While her hair was being revived, Laura, as bravely as she could, told her that Scotty was moving out that evening.

"What am I going to do without him?" Laura sobbed.

"What do you mean?" Anita sprang back. "You do what all of us lonely hearts do. You keep on going. Don't you know there's someone out there looking for you, someone with the mind, heart, and compassion worthy of a great gal like you? At least, that's what my mom keeps telling me. Now come on."

Laura looked into the mirror and wiped away a tear with her hand. She liked what Anita did to her hair.

"Yeah," said Laura. "Maybe I can get something accomplished today."

Anita fired a short burst of laughter. "Yeah, right."

Later that day, Laura was thinking about what Anita had told her as she stood at the window, her hands clasped as if in prayer. *Don't you know there's someone out there looking for you, someone with the mind, heart, and compassion worthy of a great gal like you?* Scotty continued packing. The clock on the wall said it was ten o'clock, and she would be alone soon, alone for the first time in months.

She couldn't believe this was happening. Here she stood, a warm, loving creature in a silky pink nightgown she bought the other day, and her lover was getting ready to move out of her life. Why? WHY? Because she was deeply and irretrievably immersed in a search for what happened to her parents when she was an infant? It didn't make sense.

But maybe it did. Phone calls in the middle of the night. E-mails from detectives. Secret meetings with strangers. Copies of documents culled from police academies, victims' organizations, and law enforcement agencies scattered around the apartment, plus magazines and newspapers, all fruits of her search for answers to questions that refused to go away. What happened that night? Who would want to kill her mother? Why? How was this terrible deed done in one of the safest parts of the city? What, if anything, did her father have to do with the crime? And, always, that haunting question: If he didn't kill her, why did he run away and leave his baby daughter behind?

Perhaps it was better that Scotty had made up his mind to leave and move in with his old college chum. The search for information was sapping too much of her energy and creating too many distractions in their relationship. It was also cutting into her time at work, which did not escape a few people at the ad agency, including Anita.

Finally, Scotty was done. His T-shirt drenched with sweat,

he yanked open a can of beer and downed it. "Well, I'm off," he announced.

Laura walked toward him. "Call me when you get settled," she whispered.

"Sure, and if you need anything ... anything ..." They kissed briefly. "I hope you find everything you're looking for," he added.

"Me, too." She tried to hold it together as he backed away from her.

A duffel bag, bulging in all directions, in one hand and a suitcase in the other, he walked to the door. Then, turning around, he said, "I'll be back next week for the rest of my things."

"Sure."

After he left, she threw herself on the bed and wept.

Ten minutes later, the phone rang. She was sniffling when she answered it.

"I guess he's gone," said Anita.

For the next thirty minutes, Anita did most of the talking, sharing her views on everything from a new bathing suit she'd bought to the latest news from the Middle East. "You think we have problems," she concluded.

"Yeah," Laura agreed. "Listen, I've got to go now, Anita. I'll see you tomorrow. Thanks for calling."

"Keep your chin up, don't let the bedbugs bite, et cetera, et cetera."

Two minutes after Laura hung up, the phone rang again. For a moment, she was going to ignore it, but she couldn't resist snapping it up. "HELLO!"

"Geez, somebody had a bad day," said a husky voice.

"Who's this?"

"Hi, Laura, this is Richie, Richie Frisco. I've been tryin' to reach you for the past half-hour or so."

"Sorry about that, Richie."

"No problem, sweetie. Listen, can we meet tomorrow morning? I got some information for you."

"Sure."

They settled on a diner on Eleventh Avenue.

The next morning, Richie Frisco was already eating when Laura entered the small neighborhood eatery. Richie, who was sitting in the last booth, waved when he saw her and welcomed her with genuine concern. "Hope you're in a better mood this mornin'. "

"Sorry about that. Boyfriend problems," she explained.

Richie appeared to understand. "It happens."

Without his encouragement, Laura ordered a plain toasted bagel with cream cheese and a coffee. He was eating a full breakfast of scrambled eggs, bacon, home fries, and whole grain toast. He was already on his third cup of coffee. "You eat like a sparrow," he commented when her breakfast arrived.

"More like Big Bird," she corrected him.

"If you're referrin' to your height, I like big women," he shot back. "You should see my mama."

"Your mother?"

"No, my wife."

Laura laughed, the first time in days. She felt comfortable talking with her new friend from the West Side. "What's up, Richie? Why did you want to see me?"

"I heard from my contact."

"Who?"

"Better we don't say names," he replied, pitching some eggs into his mouth. Then, gulping some coffee, he added, "Just for the sake of conversation, let's call him Vinnie, even though that's not his name. Now, Vinnie is someone I'd swear by, an old pal—well, someone I've known for a long time.

"What I'm tryin' to say is, I believe it when he tells me somethin', and, according to Vinnie, there's a guy in the neighborhood who can provide an open-and-shut alibi for your father on the night your mother was killed. Now, no one is saying the guy is a saint. In fact, he's a first-class ... bum, with a history of loan-sharking, extortion, some drugs here and there, not to mention a rotten temper."

Laura raised her hand to interrupt. "How much of this can I use without getting you or your friend in trouble?"

"Use your discretion, however you want to use it," he replied.

"This guy I'm talkin' about is dangerous. They should have locked him up and thrown away the keys years ago. I don't know how he's managed to stay out of a jail. Must be payin' off someone. His name is Lacey, Ned Lacey."

Laura almost choked on her bagel when she heard the name. Wasn't he the same guy who tried to reach her through Aunt Sally? Detective Rios also said he was a dangerous character.

Richie continued, "He has his own demolition business."

It was the same guy!

"It's small potatoes, mom and pop, compared to some of the big guys, but he seems to be doing pretty well. He lives in a garden co-op near Eighth Avenue with his wife Frances."

Richie stopped eating. He seemed to be entering another time zone. "Ah, Frances!" he went on. "Now, there's one beautiful person. I remember her when we were growing up. She was a doll, a real beauty. Everyone loved her, includin' your dad. In fact, they had something goin' there for a while. I don't know what happened between Lorney and Frances, but they broke up. Then Ned came into her life, and he made sure no one else would. Know what I mean?"

He continued, "Eventually, Frances and Ned got married and they had a son, Robby. A couple of years ago, there were reports Ned and Robby didn't get along. In fact, they were always fightin', and one night, in a drunken rage, Ned beat Robby to a pulp with a hockey stick, and the poor kid took off like a bat outta hell. That was a year ago, and Robby hasn't been seen since. But Frances has never given up hope. Every day she sits by the window, waitin' for Robby to come home."

Laura shook her head sympathetically.

"Yeah," said Richie. "Nice guy."

He continued, "Ned's got a younger brother Reggie, who's spent the better part of the past ten years or so in prison. Armed robbery. He's out now and lookin' for a job. It wouldn't surprise me if he winds up workin' for his brother, even though there's no love lost between them."

"So, what can Ned Lacey tell me that I don't know already?" she continued.

"I wish I could say exactly," Richie said. "I'm workin' on it."

Laura took a couple of sips of coffee, trying to make sense out of this new information. Then, she decided to reexamine something Richie had told her about the first time they met. "Tell me about that night again. Tell me about my father."

Richie heaved a sigh. "Well, I never saw him like that. He was always a fun-lovin' guy who loved to be with people and share a few good laughs. That night, I never saw him so down. All he kept saying was, 'She deserves better. She needs someone who can take better care of her.' Everyone tried to cheer him up. Russ Chaney, who owned the place, was cracking one joke after another; he even made your father something to eat, but ... Holy shit! You won't believe who just walked into the joint."

Laura was tempted to turn around, but didn't. "Who?"

"Himself. Ned Lacey." Richie relayed his every move to Laura.

Lacey walked to the counter and ordered a large black coffee and a buttered roll. He was probably heading back to the office after his early morning rounds at one of his sites. Laura saw fear in Richie's eyes, but he acted as if he had not noticed Lacey and kept on talking. At the same time, Laura was praying the man would not walk to the back of the diner.

Picking up the *New York Post,* Lacey glanced back at Richie, gave a quick wave, and started to walk out. Then, apparently changing his mind, he turned around and headed toward the back of the diner. Richie leapt out of his chair and rushed to meet Lacey before he reached their table.

"Nice to see you, Ned," he said.

"Likewise, Richie. Just want to tell you that if you or any of your pals are looking for work, I'm starting a new job over on Forty-sixth Street next week."

"That's real nice of you, Ned."

"Sure, just come by the office and see Gracie." Lacey tried to get a good look at Richie's table companion, but Richie blocked his view.

Richie reached out to shake Lacey's hand. "I'll spread the word," he said. Lacey once again moved toward the door.

"He's gone," Richie muttered when he returned to the table.

Laura rose. "I've got to go."

"Me, too," said the short, round man, fear still hanging over him.

Outside, Laura bent over and hugged Richie. "Thanks for the information. That was very thoughtful, and brave, of you to tell me," she said, kissing him on the cheek.

"Be careful, sweetie," he warned her.

"You, too." She walked up the block to Tenth Avenue. On the corner , she saw an empty taxi waiting for the light to turn green. Was her luck finally changing? As she prepared to enter the cab, a balding, barrel-chested man darted in front of her and swung open the door in a showy gesture of politeness.

"Oh, thank you," said Laura. The man was of medium height with dull, brown eyes staring out of milky pools streaked with patches of red. He wore a short-sleeve shirt stained with sweat along with dusty, light blue jeans.

"My pleasure," said the stocky man, forcing a crooked smile across his beefy, tanned face.

18

WHEN LAURA ARRIVED AT WORK, SHE CALLED Detective Rios to relay the information she picked up from Richie. He didn't seem impressed.

"We already questioned Ned Lacey," he said.

"How long ago was that?" she persisted

"What's the difference?" Rios replied. "It's on the record. He says he doesn't know anything about the whereabouts of your father that night."

"He's lying."

"He says he was home sleeping, sick with the flu, and his wife backs up his story," he continued.

"Then they're both lying," Laura insisted.

Rios sighed. "Without more proof, we can't do much except go back and talk to them and see if their story has changed."

"Well that's a start," she accepted. "Give me time, I'll find something."

"Let me know when you do," said Rios.

"Thanks for the vote of confidence." She hung up.

Laura looked up from her desk. Standing there was Uncle Roger, a yellow folder in his hand. Trying to regain her composure, she got up and gave him a warm hug and kiss on the cheek. "Well, this is a surprise. How are you?"

"Fine," he replied. "Hope I didn't catch you at a bad time."

"Oh, no! You're just what the doctor ordered."

He sat down. "Well, that's me, Dr. Kent," he said, a weak smile crossing his tired face. "Actually, I'm here to show you some retirement papers. I'd like you to look them over for me. Medical stuff. Maybe you can figure out what they're trying to say."

"Sure, just leave them with me."

"Now, what can I do for you?"

Laura hesitated for a moment, then said, "I think I'm getting closer. I have some new information that can place my father somewhere else when my mother was murdered."

Uncle Roger leaned back in the chair and folded his hands behind his head. "What kind of information?"

She told him what Richie Frisco had told her.

Uncle Roger stroked his chin. "How trustworthy is the source, and how trustworthy is the information?"

"I trust Richie. He's a good friend of my father's."

"I know Richie Frisco and I know Ned Lacey. They're no angels, either one, especially that Lacey guy. What makes you think Lacey will tell you anything new? I mean, if he didn't say anything before, why should he say anything now?"

Laura shrugged her shoulders.

"And don't you think you ought to turn the information over to the detective on the case?"

"I did."

"And?"

"He'll go back and talk to Lacey and his wife. Maybe."

Anita came into the office. "Oops! I didn't know you entertained handsome men so early in the morning," she said with a deadpan face. When Roger didn't smile, she rolled her large dark eyes and added, "Sorry. Just a little morning humor."

"Meet my friend, Anita Tedesco," said Laura. "This is my Uncle Roger."

"Oh, hi, Uncle Roger," said Anita, shaking his hand robustly. "I heard about you."

"Was it good?"

"Actually, it wasn't half bad for a cop .... oh, sorry, police officer." Roger smiled. "See, I knew he had great teeth," said Anita, adding, "Just came by to tell you the boss man called a meeting, ASAP. Bring all your stuff on the Shepley campaign."

Roger got up to go. He reached over and kissed Laura on the cheek. "We'll talk more later," he said. "Just be careful. Aunt Sally's really worried about you. So am I. Please, don't do anything risky." He looked over at Anita, then back at Laura. "If you ever need any help, just call me." He left.

"Wow, that was a bit dire," Anita remarked.

"Yeah," said Laura. "He's always been a worrier." One of her earliest memories was being in a playground with her uncle He watched her like a hawk, barking out all these commands. "Watch out." "Stop running." "Don't climb up there." "You're gonna fall." Being a very curious child, she wanted to explore and try new things, just like the big kids, but when her uncle minded her in the playground she felt terrified, immobilized.

"Oh, he's alright. Just a little protective," Laura added.

"Hey, what do you expect?" said Anita.

"Yeah, I guess," said Laura. "Anyway, I remember, when I was six or seven, and we were at Jones Beach. I got lost, or so they said. Well, you'd think the President was kidnapped. He corralled a few of his police buddies, who happened to be with us that day, and they started fanning out all over the beach searching for me."

"Well, I guess they found you. You're here."

"Actually, I wasn't lost," explained Laura. "I was three blankets away playing in the sand with a nice, little Hispanic kid I met that day. When they—the boy and his mom—got up to go home, I just went back to my blanket. Aunt Sally was gazing out into the ocean looking for me or my body. She almost squashed me to death with the hugs when she saw me."

"Is she a worry-wart, too?"

"Worse," Laura continued. "She's a drill sergeant. Used to ask me a hundred questions every day when I was a teenager. Actually, I was a pretty good kid, but she kept close tabs on me. She still does."

"Just like your mom would."

Laura nodded. She looked out the window and watched

Uncle Roger exit the front door, light up a cigarette, and head off downtown to his precinct. She continued, "They kept me out of harm's way, that's for sure. Maybe they were a bit much, but, you know what, in a way it was comforting. We were family. We had some fun times together, too, especially when we were sitting around the table at home. My uncle was a Mets fan, I was a Yankee fan, and we used to have some good, healthy debates, statistics flying all over the place. It was my way of showing I had a brain."

She paused, then added. "Looking back now, I think I know why they were so protective. After what happened to my parents, they didn't want anything to happen to me."

"Did they ever talk to you about them?"

"Sure," said Laura, "when I got older. For a long time, they didn't tell me anything—they probably didn't want to upset me—but when I kept pressing them, they opened up. They know as much as anyone who read the papers back then, and they are convinced that my dad couldn't, didn't, kill my mom."

"Interesting," said Anita, looking at her watch. "Oh, oh. Boss man is calling."

Across town, Ned Lacey also had a meeting to attend. When he arrived at his office, his brother Reggie was already there, sitting behind his desk and flipping a pencil in the air. The look on Ned's face told him to get up and move to another chair, which he did. Ned sat down, took the lid off his coffee and took a bite into his buttered roll.

"I could've skipped the roll, but thanks for the coffee," said Reggie. A smile tried to mask the sarcasm, but did a bad job of it.

Ned shrugged his shoulders. So many people had said they resembled each other. Yet, there was Ned, behind the desk, calling the shots, and here was Reggie, his hat in his hand, waiting for a handout. Ned had called him to his office today to give him the handout of a lifetime.

"A month ago, you got out of prison," Ned began. "Now you're looking to get as far away from here as possible ... and why not? You still got a lot of living to do."

Reggie gave a slight nod.

"Just look around the neighborhood," Ned continued. "I mean, do you recognize the place anymore? Foreign restaurants everywhere ... high-rises ... pricey apartments in newly renovated buildings. We used to call them tenements ... skyrocketing prices ... Ah, it's nuts!"

A puzzled look slipped across Reggie's face.

"Anyway," Ned continued, "I know that your patience is wearing thin. You've got a dream, but you need cash, lots of it, to make it come true. And you know better than I that you can't afford to pull another caper and risk being a three-time loser, right? I think I can help you and Milly. Mama always said big brother should take care of little brother."

Reggie squirmed in his chair, disdain in his face. There was no such thing as brotherly love between these brothers. "I'm listening."

19

As she did every Tuesday evening, Anita Tedesco was minding her six-year-old niece, Madeline, at a playground in Queens. Anita just loved spending time with the girl—one-on-one, godmother to niece, no parents allowed—even if it meant she'd wind up in a playground on a hot, humid evening.

How she envied her brother and sister-in-law. They had a family! Deep down she always felt she'd make a great mother. But, as she neared thirty, that prospect appeared to be slipping away. Oh, there were plenty of relationships in the past, some lasting as long as two years. But, for some reason, they always fizzled. Most of the time, it was Anita who wanted out. Nevertheless, she remained hopeful, as did her mother, who urged her to be steadfast. "Don't worry, sweetheart, there's a man out there with your name on him," she'd tell her,

From a bench, Anita tried to keep a close eye on Madeline without looking too anxious or protective. A tall, lithe woman in gray shorts sat down next to her. "They play well together, don't they?" said the woman, referring to Madeline and her son, Oliver. "Yeah," Anita replied.

"I'm Jenny, Oliver's mother," said the woman, gesturing toward the boy in pursuit of Madeline around the slides. "Are you Madeline's mother?"

"Nah, I'm her aunt. Anita's my name."

"Married?"

Anita turned and faced the woman. "Not yet, working on it. Right now, I'm working my ass off in the city all week long," she said, a bit of annoyance in her voice.

She didn't wait for the woman's reaction. Oliver was running toward his mother. "Mama, mama, Madeline is talking to a stranger behind the fence."

Anita leapt off the bench and ran to the area behind the slides. Madeline was standing by a low fence there, staring at a man in the distance running toward the parking lot. "What happened?" asked Anita anxiously. "Did he hurt you?"

"No, Aunt Anita," the girl explained. "The man said he wanted to buy me ice cream. I told him to get lost, just like you told me."

Anita leaned over and kissed Madeline on the cheek. "Good girl." Then, her eyes ablaze with fury, she screamed at the figure getting into a car, "You better run, you piece of shit!"

On hearing that, parents scooped up their kids and dashed out of the playground. Among the evacuees were the lithe mother in gray shorts and Oliver.

"He wanted me to give you this," said Madeline, handing Anita a folded piece of paper. She opened it. The message was short:

> *Tell your friend to back off NOW!*
> *Like mother, like daughter?*
> THE HOUND OF HELL

The message was short, but clear. Anita knew she had no choice but to convey it to Laura.

When Laura heard, she was more worried about what had happened—that Anita's six-year-old niece had been placed in danger—than about the message. There were too many good people who could be hurt now. "Bottom line," said Laura when Anita called her that evening, "someone out there wants me to mind my own business, but this *IS* my business, and I'm *NOT* going to stop nosing around! I can't!"

"I know," said Anita.

"But please, please, Anita," Laura continued, her voice cracking. "I'm worried about you and everyone close to me. Do yourself and me a favor. Stay as far away from me as possible."

"Yeah, like friends can stop being friends," Anita snapped. "You do what you feel you have to do, but be careful! I can take care of myself."

At work the next day, Laura exchanged knowing glances and small talk with Anita, but avoided any mention of the playground incident. Luckily, Laura was called to an important production shoot. It kept her busy all day and helped her put some of her personal concerns on hold. Once in a while, she'd think about what Richie had told her.

20

For Richie Frisco, it was no different than any other hot summer evening.

When dinner was over, he got up from the table and headed toward the front door. "See you later, hon," he alerted his wife, who was in the kitchen.

Julie, a tall, substantial woman in her early fifties who had survived breast cancer, stopped doing what she was doing and walked into the living room. "Where're you going?" she asked, brushing aside wispy light brown hair.

He pointed his index finger toward the roof. He loved to retire to the roof at the end of a hot day and look out over the sweltering city as it shimmered into its nightclothes. If he were lucky, he'd catch an errant breeze to offset the stale smell of garbage or yesterday's rain. Perhaps he'd even spot a majestic hawk sailing high overhead in the early evening sky.

"They say it's going to rain," she said.

"I'll take my chances."

Julie folded her hands gently around his neck. "Don't worry so much, Richie. I'm sure she'll be alright," she said, referring to Laura Bennett. She knew her husband was concerned about the young woman's safety in light of the new information he gave her. "From what you tell me, she sounds like one tough babe. She won't let anyone rattle her cage, and she's smart enough not to do anything stupid."

"I hope," he said, kissing his wife.

Richie walked out the front door and up the first of four flights of stairs. The farther he climbed, the more he felt the heat of the day collecting in the upper cavities of the five-story building. On the third flight of stairs, he stopped to rest. Damn! How often had his wife reminded him, "We got to do somethin' about this weight." Tomorrow he would start. He would begin eating more sensibly and exercising. Slapping his potbelly in disgust, Richie resumed his climb to the summit of what seemed like Mount Everest. Sweat poured off of him in rivulets as he reached the final flight of stairs. He stopped once again and sat down, any memory of climbing the stairs two steps at a time fading like the sunlight.

Suddenly, from deep within the bowels of the building, he heard a voice calling after him. It was Julie. "Richie, Richie, are you there yet?"

He gasped for air. Finally he answered her. "Almost. I'm almost there. What is it?"

"You have a phone call."

"Who is it?"

"I don't know."

"Get a name and number. I'll call back."

"Okay. Don't be long. It's hot up there."

"I know, I know," he muttered, incredulous.

"What's that, honey?"

"I SAID I KNOW IT'S HOT UP HERE."

"Why are you yelling?"

Sometimes she just didn't seem to understand him, and the communications gap only seemed to be widening since their son Tommy left home to join the army. He and Tommy were more like brothers than father and son. They did so many things together, from crabbing on the Jersey shore to going to Rangers games. Since Tommy was deployed overseas, Richie felt lost without his buddy. Only his recent involvement as a coach of a neighborhood baseball team for pre-teens shook him out of the doldrums.

As he opened the roof door, a gentle breeze welcomed him,

and he showed his appreciation by taking several deep breaths. He was surprised to catch a faint odor of tobacco smoke in the air, as if someone had just lit up, and he looked around to see if there was anyone on the roof or the connecting roofs. There was no one in sight except for a couple of teenagers, a boy and a girl, who appeared to be kissing against a chimney wall two buildings away. That brought back some pleasant memories for Richie. The young couple stopped kissing, turned toward him, and waved. He waved back, slightly embarrassed.

Richie walked to the edge of the roof for a closer look at the neighborhood he loved. How Hell's Kitchen was changing! On tree-lined streets, old tenements that had housed desperately poor residents were being renovated and giving way to upscale apartment or condo complexes for professionals, performers, and other climbers. Many of his old friends had moved out, to Jersey or the Island, but there was still a core of old faces lingering in high-rises and rent-stabilized apartments.

The sun's last rays were skipping across skyscrapers and setting windows ablaze. Once again, a warm breeze embraced him, and there was that whiff of tobacco in the air. Richie turned around, but saw no one behind him. High above, he saw what his heart was looking for: A hawk soaring splendidly in the sky. For a moment, he felt at peace with himself and the world, when a tremendous force knocked his breath away and sent him reaching for a lifeline in the wind.

When Laura left work that day, the sun was starting to set, and a purplish haze bathed a hot, steamy city. Heavy clouds were rolling in from the Southwest, promising a thunderstorm or two. She couldn't help noticing a lone bird, probably a hawk, gliding high overhead. She decided to walk home, despite the threat of rain.

Down one of the side streets, she saw a tall man in a cowboy hat unloading a van. From the back, he looked like Scotty, and she was tempted to say hello. He took off his hat and wiped the sweat that was beading on his brow, and gave her a big, warm smile. She smiled back as she walked past him. As she did, she wondered whether she had done the right thing. Smiling at strangers on a lonely street in a darkening city!

Near home, Laura decided to keep the custom she shared with Scotty on Wednesdays and went to their favorite Chinese restaurant.

"The usual, Miss Bennett?" inquired the owner, a short woman, her dark eyes offering a friendly welcome.

"Yes"

"Egg Drop Soup and Wu Se Gai Zee ... for two?"

"Make that for one, Li, and I'll eat it here."

"Oh, Mr. Scotty out of town?" asked the woman, her hair rolled up into a bun.

`Laura didn't feel like going into details. "Sort of," she winced.

While she waited for the food, she took out the papers Uncle Roger left with her. She tried to make sense out of them, but she wasn't ready to decode the language—"Coverage Options," "Medically Necessary Services," "Identity Theft". She had other things on her mind. She took out a pad and began making notes.

Ned Lacey—demolition, dangerous

Wife Frances—waiting for son to return

Son Robby—ran away after fight with Ned

Reggie—young brother, just out of jail

Ned and Reggie–no love lost

Dad and Ned–the connection?

Her food arrived, and she began eating, quickly at first as she tried to put the pieces together, then more slowly. All of a sudden, she ducked, as if she were trying to avoid a blow; the sky exploded with a thunderous roar. When the rain started falling in buckets, Li came over to the table and calmly said, "Not to worry, Ms. Bennett. I give you umbrella to use."

Laura thanked her and continued eating. Something had struck her about the way Richie Frisco reacted when Ned Lacey entered the diner. He was really frightened. She could see it in his eyes. What did Richie know that he had not told her about that man? Was there something long-simmering between Richie and Lacey? Did it have anything to do with Lacey's wife Frances, whom Richie spoke so fondly of? She hardly knew what she was eating.

21

It was raining hard when Laura left the restaurant. Standing in the doorway, she considered hailing a cab, but decided against it. She was only three blocks away from home and armed with Li's umbrella. Besides, the rain was a refreshing change from a heat wave that was in its fourth day.

After the phone calls, the scaffolding incident, and the playground warning, Laura paused several times along the way and turned around to see if anyone was following her. When she saw no one, she resumed her quick pace.

Drawing near her apartment complex, she looked up at that all too familiar and frightening building under construction. In the driving rain, she hurried around it into the middle of the street. As she did, a pickup truck, its lights blazing, came barreling down the street toward her. For a brief moment, she froze. Then, with a quickness she had not shown since she played high school basketball, she leapt onto the sidewalk. Unfortunately, Li's umbrella didn't make it. It was crushed under the truck's wheels, which never stopped rolling.

As she lay on the sidewalk frozen with fear, Laura's eyes followed the truck down the street, but she could not make out the license plate number in the heavy rain. After she managed to get on her feet, she limped into the lobby and looked around.

Charlie the doorman was nowhere in sight. *Where is he when you need him?* She went directly to the elevator and up to her apartment.

Flopping on the sofa, drenched and sore, she was thankful she was still alive, but she couldn't help wondering. Was the truck a missile intentionally aimed at her by someone who wanted her dead or did she just happen to be in the way of one of those mad drivers hell-bent on seeing how fast a truck can go in the rain? She shivered at both possibilities, while she resolved to buy Li a new umbrella tomorrow.

The phone rang. Fear mingled with a burning curiosity as she snapped it up. "WHO'S THIS?" she fired out.

"Hell, you don't have to take my head off. It's just me."

"Oh, hi, Uncle Roger. Sorry."

"No problem. You okay?"

"I'm fine. What's up?"

"I just thought I'd call to finish up our conversation from this morning," he replied. "I tried calling you a couple of times earlier."

"I was out ... worked late, stopped for dinner, Chinese ... and oh, Uncle Roger, I'm so tired and worn out ..."

"Are you alright?"

She proceeded to tell him about her long day at the office, the walk home from the restaurant, and the drenching rain, but she decided not to say anything about the truck that almost killed her. Otherwise, he'd be running over.

"Just glad to be home," she concluded.

When she finished, there was a silence that hung out there longer than she would have hoped. "Have you turned on the TV?" he said finally.

"Why, what's happening?" said Laura.

He hesitated. "Oh, just some more bad news from the Middle East," he replied, adding, "Please, let me come over."

"No, Uncle Roger, I just want to take a bath and go to bed."

"Are you sure?"

"Yes."

"Alright," he said, resigned. "Just call if you need me. Like I told you before, be careful."

When she hung up, she went into the bathroom and drew a bath. After undressing, she slipped into the tub and closed her eyes, the cares of the day stubbornly refusing to let go. Drip, drip, drip. A leaking faucet was no match for the drenching rain beating against the small round window over the tub, but together they provided soothing therapeutic sounds. Five minutes, ten minutes passed, and she was beginning to feel more relaxed, and sleepy.

Suddenly, the intercom buzzed, and a man's voice came over it, invading her private world. Laura wasn't sure what it was saying at first.

She sprang out of the tub, threw on a bathrobe, and walked into the foyer.

"What is it, Charlie?"

"Someone to see you, Ms. Bennett," the doorman announced.

"Who is it?" Laura inquired.

"A Detective Rios, ma'am, badge and all."

"Give me five minutes and send him up. Thanks, Charlie."

Laura ran around furiously looking for something to wear. She put on a tired pair of jeans and an old sweatshirt and started brushing her hair when the doorbell rang. This would be her first face-to-face meeting with the man who took over her mother's murder case. Sliding into sneakers, she opened the door.

She was surprised by what she saw. Somehow she thought Detective Rios would be taller, muscles bulging through the seams of a sloppy, light gray suit. Instead, he was a thin man of average height dressed to kill in a striped, dark blue suit, and he was very handsome. Lively but sad dark eyes set against a soft, tawny complexion surveyed her apartment, or what he could see of it, at the doorway. A thin moustache gave him the finish of a maitre d' in a fine restaurant.

Laura could not tell what was going on behind the façade, but she had a feeling this was a man in crisis. She put on her best smile and held out her hand. "It's nice to meet you, Detective."

"Yes, yes, indeed," he replied, taking her hand and flashing a smile that disappeared as quickly as it appeared. "I wish it were under better circumstances."

She noticed the change in his appearance with some anxiousness. She led him into the apartment. "Sit down. Would you like something to drink? Water, soda, coffee?"

"No, I'm good."

She leaned back in her chair, trying to hide the fear that lurked just below the surface. "What's going on?" she asked.

"It's about Richie Frisco."

She took a deep breath, expecting the worst.

He continued, wasting no time to report the news. "He was found dead earlier this evening."

Laura suddenly felt sick and faint, and a deep, throbbing pain exploded in the front of her head. She wanted to scream and cry, but knew she needed to compose herself to get the full story. After all, Richie was a man in seemingly good health and spirits when she shared breakfast with him only that morning. "What happened?" she asked through glistening eyes.

"We don't know for sure. This old couple, they were walking their dog when they heard a thud on the sidewalk. When they turned around and saw a man lying there, moaning, they called the police. The ambulance came but it was too late. It happened a little after eight o'clock. His wife, who was in their apartment at the time, almost collapsed when she heard the news, but managed to tell us that Richie quite frequently went up to the roof after dinner. It was his way of relaxing, she says."

It sounded like something Richie would do. "So what happened?" she asked.

"We don't know yet for sure," he said. "His wife says there was a phone call for Richie when he was walking up the stairs to the roof. She didn't recognize the voice, a man's, but she says whoever called had hung up when she got back"

Rios continued, "We checked the roof. No structural damage or problems there as far as we could see. His wife says Richie was very sure-footed, so it's not likely he accidentally fell off the roof, but it's possible. Did he have a heart attack and collapse? No way, she says. He just had a complete physical and was given a clean bill of health. The coroners will confirm that. There's the possibility he jumped, but once again his wife says No; he would never do anything like that. He was looking forward to coaching in a playoff game this weekend."

"Could he have been pushed?" asked Laura.

"Right now, it looks like an accident to us," he replied, "but this could change."

Rios was silent for a moment, then continued, "I'm telling you all of this because I believe you had nothing to do with what happened to Richie."

Laura was trembling now, a mixture of grief, guilt, and anger welling inside her. She got up and walked toward the window. "Jesus, don't you remember what I told you this morning?" she raged. "Maybe if you'd acted ..."

"Please, Ms. Bennett ..."

"Please, nothing. Why didn't you follow up on my lead?"

Rios sighed. "We did talk to Ned Lacey before *and* after Richie was found dead. He stuck by his story about your father's whereabouts. And he says he was at a prizefight tonight, which was confirmed by a couple of guys."

"Then, who? WHO DID THIS?"

"At this point, we don't know if anybody did it," he replied. "Our team is looking at all of the possibilities." He hesitated, then added, "I can't emphasize this enough: You have to be extremely careful, Ms. Bennett. You've put yourself in harm's way, and ..."

She seemed far away. "Ned Lacey knows something. I just know it! I just know it!" she mumbled.

Rios got up and handed her his card. "Here's my cell number." He headed for the door. "Call me anytime ... anytime. I'll keep someone posted outside the building here."

"No," she said. "I'll be fine."

He shook his head and walked out into the hallway. She shut the door after him and locked it. The ache in her head was piercing now, and she hadn't told him about the truck incident. She had no idea what to do next.

PART 5

BATS AND BYGONES

22

It was Friday, and Laura was physically and emotionally drained when she left work. She purposely didn't stop to chat with Charlie as she often did when she entered the lobby where she lived. All she wanted to do was get upstairs, take a soothing bath, and go to bed. It had been an incredibly difficult two days, following Richie's death.

The phone was ringing when she entered the apartment. Laura reluctantly picked it up.

Detective Rios was on the other end.

"I just wanted to let you know that we've had another sighting, this time in Las Vegas," he told her. "Seems that your dad was on the move again after living under an assumed name—Peter Fox—in Arizona."

"Do you know where he was headed?"

"No."

"Where was he living in Arizona?"

"His residence was traced to a small, rented house in Mesa," he replied. "Local police checked out the place. A man called Peter Fox *was* living there, but he was gone when police arrived. The manager who rented the house said that this Peter Fox had called him and said he had to leave in a hurry. There was 'an emergency in the family.'"

"That's more than we learned from any other sighting," she observed.

"I suppose so," said Rios.

"Well, at least he may be alive," she concluded.

"It's a lead," he noted. "I thought you should know about it."

Laura sensed a little more concern in his voice than she had heard the last time they talked. "Thanks, Detective."

At the same time, ten thousand miles in the air, Billy Volpe seemed calm and relaxed as his 747 approached Kennedy International Airport. Actually, his heart was pounding with excitement. It had been a long time, nearly fourteen years, since he had been in New York City. The last time, he had come to explore some promising job opportunities at a couple of newspapers, or so he told his parents, but actually he went there for a secret rendezvous with his sweetheart, Trudi Dineen. It was a magical four days.

Now, here he was, on his way back to the scene of that memorable tryst, but with an entirely different goal. Was he doing the right thing? Was he putting himself and his daughter at risk by traveling more than two-thousand miles to let a young woman he never met know that they had spent an afternoon with her fugitive father, the prime suspect in the murder of her mother? More important, how would Laura react to hearing that they had found her father to be a kind, engaging man? Something told Billy that if she were anything like her dad, she would welcome the news, but who knows? That was the chance he was willing to take.

In the seat next to him, Alex was still clutching the arm rests for dear life. "We should be landing soon," he assured her. She could hardly contain her excitement. In a few minutes, she would be in the storied home of so many of her favorite things, including cannoli, the New York Yankees, and *CSI: New York*, which her father sometimes let her watch with him.

They finally landed. On the way to the hotel, both Billy and Alex looked out the taxi window at the jagged line of tall buildings that formed the famous New York skyline. Their enthusiasm only intensified with the heavy traffic snarls slowing their progress.

When they finally reached Manhattan and moved toward the midtown area, Billy turned to Alex. "Some town, huh?" he said.

Alex nodded.

"It's like coming back home, to my roots," he beamed. Alex flipped her eyes upward. Apparently she knew what was coming next. He had told the story many times before.

"You know, my mom and dad were born in the Bronx, just up the road from here," he continued, no matter that streets are seldom referred to as roads by New Yorkers. "My grandparents on both sides came here from Italy in the twenties and lived in Manhattan before getting married and moving to the Bronx."

There it was ahead of them, the Empire State Building.

"When my mom and dad got married, they lived next door to my grandparents for a while," he went on. "Then along I came. When I was three, my family moved to Detroit so that my father could take a job with Ford, and that's where we stayed until we moved to Arizona."

"My parents did the same thing," bellowed the cabdriver. "Only after we went to Detroit, we came back here. We missed the city. Most of all, we missed the bagels." His hearty laugh startled both Alex and Billy.

"Were you born in the Bronx?" asked Billy.

"You bet."

"No kidding, what part?" asked Billy.

"The bad part," he replied, letting out another bellow over his own joke. "Well, here we are, folks," he said, stopping the cab in front of a midtown hotel. "Welcome to New York."

Billy didn't waste any time unpacking when he got up to the room. He dialed her number.

Laura almost didn't pick up the phone. But after four rings she finally answered it.

"Oh hi, Ms. Bennett," said the caller. "You don't know me.

My name is Billy Volpe, and my daughter and I just arrived from Arizona."

"Uh-huh."

"I know this sounds crazy," he began nervously. "We've only landed in New York less than an hour ago. But can we meet somewhere? I have some information about your father you may be interested in hearing."

Laura wanted to hear more.

"I'm a reporter," said Billy. "I work as a stringer for several newspapers in Arizona, and as part of my job I do stories on anything that's newsworthy in and around the Phoenix area. I also take pictures."

At this point, Laura's instinct was to slam the phone down, but she didn't.

"Well, that's how I met your father," he went on. "It was purely by chance. I was assigned to cover this freak car accident in Mesa, and it happened to involve your father's car."

Mesa! Wasn't that where Rios said he had been living?

"We talked briefly at the scene of the accident, your father and I," he rambled on. "He didn't like the fact that I was taking so many pictures. I told him my editor preferred I take a lot of photos on stories he assigned. Well ..."

A new voice, a young girl's, abruptly jumped in. "Hi, Ms. Bennett. This is Alex. My dad told you how he first met your father. It's a long story, but you should know we had a chance to spend some time with him, and we both found him to be a really nice person."

"Where are you?" Laura asked.

Billy told her the name of the hotel where they were staying.

"I know it," said Laura. "There's a café in the lobby. I'll meet you there. What do you look like?"

"I have this nest on my face. My friends call me Serpico West."

"I'll see you in twenty minutes."

When Laura arrived at the café she had no trouble spotting Billy and Alex. Billy rose to greet her, a warm smile on his face.

Alex was sitting there in ponytails, her head nestled in her hand. Her face lit up when she saw Laura. "You look just like your dad," she beamed.

The sudden comparison with her father took Laura by surprise, and her face flushed with emotion.

Billy saw the change in her. "Please, Laura, please sit down. Can I order you something?"

"No ... well yes ... just a Coke."

Billy began telling her how he met her father at the scene of the accident. "It was incredible. No one was really hurt, except your father scraped his knees trying to catch up with the car."

"How did you know he was my father?" Laura asked.

Billy paused, then replied, "That's a good question. When I first met him he was using the name Peter Fox."

Oh, my God!

"But after looking at the photos taken at the accident scene," he continued, "we became suspicious, Alex and I. He looked familiar, and following our instincts, we did some investigating. Peter Fox, we discovered, had an amazing likeness to Lorne Bennett, the movie actor. Later, we tapped the Internet and found stories about your mother's murder, the suspicions raised about your father, his flight ... I can't tell you what a revelation it all was. To be honest, at first I thought I was onto the biggest story of my life, but then ... something happened."

"What happened?"

"We got to meet your father face-to-face, in Las Vegas. He went there, I think, to avoid any more publicity after the accident," Billy replied.

"We had lunch together," Alex jumped in. "We walked and talked and saw some of the sights, including the MGM lions."

Billy smiled, nodded.

"We had a great time," Alex continued. "He was nice to be around, warm, friendly, and funny, too. You should be very be very proud, Ms. Bennett."

Laura could feel years of hurt, anger, and turmoil rising to the surface. *No, stay in control. Listen to what they're saying.*

"Yes. He was a real gentleman," Billy added. "That's why I stopped thinking of him as the big story and started thinking of him as a human being. I began wondering what it was like to be on the run for twenty-two years, to be wary of everyone around you, to be alone, cut off from your family and friends. And then I started thinking about you ..."

Stay in control. Stay in control. Is it possible that this bearded man and this pretty girl in pigtails had really stumbled onto my father and talked with him and walked with him?

"How do you know that man was really my father?" she pressed them.

"Because he was," said Alex with matter-of-face innocence.

"The last time we saw him, at the airport, he knew we knew who he really was," Billy added. "I know it might have been an accident or coincidence that we ran into your father, but maybe it was more than that. Maybe we were given this opportunity to meet your father and to let you know that we saw him and he's alright. Which is why we're here."

Laura felt numb, speechless. Then, turning to Billy, she asked with piercing eyes, "Where is he? Where is he now?"

"I don't know," he replied.

Laura shook her head in disbelief. "So what's the point? If he's on the run again, why are you telling me all of this?"

Billy paused, collecting his thoughts. "I thought you'd like to know." He picked up a large manila envelope on the seat next to him. "I know all of this may sound hard to believe, but here are some photos I took at the scene of the accident. They're my copies. They're not my best work. It was late and a bit chaotic. But they might be the only pictures of your dad in twenty-two years."

He handed her the photo of her father gesturing and talking to the police. Because of the distance at which that photo was shot and the angle of her father's face, she could not get a clear picture of what he looked like, but he appeared to be a tall, handsome man, just as her aunt and uncle had described him. One by one, she studied the other photos. None offered any better views, but she was visibly moved.

Billy reached over to pat her hand. Laura pulled away, struggling not to show that she wanted to believe what these two strangers from Arizona were saying. But it was useless. Looking across the table, her hazel eyes glistening in the café light, she said, "If this is true, you don't know what this means to me. I've been searching for a long time. I have a lot of questions. Sometimes I think my father's the only one who really has the answers. That's why I want to find him. I need to find him."

"I'll never really understand what you're feeling, but I want to help," said Billy. "I want to help you any way I can," said Billy.

"Me, too," said Alex, reaching into her purse. "Would you like a tissue?" she asked.

Laura smiled, took one.

They talked for about two hours. Billy furnished more details of their meeting, and Alex turned over the gold-plated key and baby sock they found outside Lorne's house in Mesa. Laura took another look at Billy's photos. Suspicions started melting away. By the time she left to return home, Laura believed what they were saying.

23

THE NEXT DAY, LAURA TELEPHONED HER AUNT and uncle in Queens. Familiar with the Kents' Saturday routine, she cheerfully asked Uncle Roger whether it would be alright if she came by that afternoon. "I'd like you and Aunt Sally to meet a couple of friends from Arizona," she explained.

"Sure," he replied. "I hope they like barbecued spare ribs and chicken, Queens style."

"I don't know, but I'm sure it will be an experience they'll never forget," she said. "Oh, by the way, one of my friends is a twelve-year-old girl."

"Great," he teased. "I'll take the Jack Daniel's out of the barbecue sauce."

Laura laughed, glad he was in good spirits. "We'll be by in about an hour or so."

There was a reason Laura wanted to visit her aunt and uncle other than to introduce Billy and Alex. She wanted to see whether they could identify the shiny gold-plated key and baby sock they had found. She had decided not to mention this other reason to Uncle Roger over the phone. She knew what he thought about her persistent probing into her mother's murder and her father's disappearance. Such matters, he felt, were better left to the police.

Arriving at the Kents', Laura guided Billy and Alex up the driveway to the patio area where Uncle Roger was turning a rack of ribs on the grill.

"Oh, good, just in time," he said when he saw Laura and her guests. "Sal, they're here!" he shouted at the screen door.

Aunt Sally didn't have to be called twice. Swinging open the door, she was a commanding presence as she swept across the patio and kissed Laura. Aunt Sally hardly saw her niece these days, a disappointment she often shared with her friends at meetings with her church friends. After all, wasn't Laura practically her own child? "It's so nice to see you, darling. You look wonderful, maybe a little tired, but wonderful. Now introduce me to your friends. I bet you're all starving."

"Meet Billy Volpe, from Arizona. And this is his daughter, Alexandra."

Aunt Sally welcomed them with open arms. Uncle Roger, never one for hugs and kisses, shook their hands.

"Call me Alex. Everyone does," the twelve-year-old insisted.

The ribs and chicken were a hit with everyone. After they ate, Aunt Sally invited Alex for a tour of the house. Laura went along for a nostalgic look. The downstairs rooms in the old, two-story colonial-style structure were spacious, though a bit cluttered, but they seemed comfortable enough, with furniture that managed to stand the test of time. The living room was like a chapel. A large poster of the Sacred Heart welcomed all visitors, and a lit votive candle stood guard in front of it.

On the way upstairs, Aunt Sally explained who was who in the large collection of photos lining one wall. Absent were any pictures of Lorne Bennett. When they reached Laura's old bedroom, Aunt Sally—with a glance toward Laura—declared it was available whenever her niece or any of her friends wanted to use it.

When they returned to the patio, Uncle Roger was peppering Billy with questions about Arizona. When the conversation turned to Billy's experiences as a reporter-writer, Laura felt it was time to jump in. "Enough you guys." she chirped. "Enough already, I've got something to say." She paused but saw no reason for a big buildup. "Billy and Alex met my father a week ago in Arizona."

Aunt Sally blessed herself. Uncle Roger's jaw tightened, his eyes squinting with a look of suspicion about to turn to rage. "What is this some kind of con game?" he flared.

"No, Uncle Roger, I believe them," said Laura.

"I met him, Roger, I really did," Billy added.

"Yeah, right!" said Uncle Roger.

"I met him, too," said Alex, "and if it was up to me, I'd have his picture on the wall inside. I think he's a very nice man."

"I knew it was going to happen someday," Aunt Sally murmured.

Uncle Roger rose from the table. "I gotta go to work."

"Wait, please," said Laura. She reached into her purse and pulled out the sock and key. "These were found outside the house where he was living in Arizona. Do they look familiar?"

Uncle Roger shook his head, disgusted, and walked into the house. Aunt Sally made a move to follow him, then sat back and stared at the two items on the table. Laura came over and put her hand on her shoulder.

"No need to be nervous, Aunt Sally," said Laura. "I know this is all a shock, and Uncle Roger will get over it. Please, just take a moment and see if you can recognize these things."

"They don't look familiar," she stammered.

Now, it was Alex's turn. "Try again, Aunt Sally," the girl pleaded. "Anything come to mind?"

They could hear Uncle Roger starting up his car and driving off to work. Aunt Sally shook her head sullenly. "I hate to see him go to work upset. You know how important doing a good job is to your uncle."

They waited for Aunt Sally to turn her attention back to the items on the table.

"I don't know, I don't know," she said.

The change in her demeanor was noticeable. Gone was the bubbly self-confidence that had greeted Laura and her two friends when they arrived earlier that afternoon. Aunt Sally seemed lost, frightened. Laura was aware of the change, but she persisted. "Please, Aunt Sally, concentrate."

"The key, I never saw it before," Aunt Sally mumbled. "This

looks like a baby sock, and it has a distinctive design ... It could have been yours when you were a baby, Laura, but I don't know for sure. It's been a long time."

"But what would my father be doing with my sock?" Laura asked.

"He kept it because it reminded him of you," Alex suggested.

"And could the key have some connection with the past, too?" asked Billy.

The silence that followed lasted only seconds, but it seemed forever. Aunt Sally finally broke it. "As far as I'm concerned, the past is over, gone forever," she began, "but if it's the past you want ..."

Laura put her arm around her aunt's shoulders. "What are you trying to say, Aunt Sally?"

"If it's the past you want," she continued flatly, "it's down the basement. That's where Uncle Roger put Aurora's personal things, with all the junk he's collected over the years. You know Uncle Roger. He doesn't throw out anything."

"If you don't mind, Aunt Sally, I'd like to take a look," said Laura.

Aunt Sally reflected on her response, then said, "It's a mess, a real pit, down there. Scares me to death. God knows what's down there—spiders, bugs, bats. Not much light. The only one who goes down there these days is your uncle. I haven't been in the basement in months."

"I'll bring a flashlight," Laura said.

24

Aunt Sally was right. The basement was a pit, a dimly lit hole in the ground filled with large and small bags, boxes, and odd pieces of furniture choking under a thick layer of dust and the smell of mildew. Hanging from steam pipes were old plant pots waiting for new plants, clothes hangers holding garments faintly visible through dirty see-through plastic wraps, along with Halloween masks, Christmas wreathes, a battered child-sized swimming pool, and a pink and green girl's bike with one wheel missing. Laura recognized some of the things.

Two narrow paths led away from the stairway through the collection of rejects, junk, and old memories. One went to a small room that was neatly organized by someone who took pride in the arsenal of household tools assembled there. "Uncle Roger always took very good care of his things," Laura explained.

The other led to the far end of the basement, into a room that was separated from the main room by a wood-paneled wall. Laura knew it as Uncle Roger's room, and no one was allowed to enter it and mess up things. Billy brushed up against a string and pulled it, and a dim light went on overhead. A blue tarpaulin lay over more than half of the room, covering objects of various shapes and sizes.

Laura and Billy removed the tarp. Under it were neatly stacked cardboard boxes, plastic containers, a cherry mahogany chest, and other small pieces of furniture that, remarkably, looked new and shiny, as though they were delivered to the house that day. Laura took a deep breath, fighting back an overwhelming feeling of anticipation and excitement. She bent over the chest and lifted the lid. It opened easily, without a key.

She stared down at the contents—neatly folded tablecloths, napkins, and other linen along with a collection of fine silverware in a handsome wooden box with the word *Bennett* carved on the top. Laura gently picked up a fork and a spoon, then a napkin, which she held to her cheek. This was the first time she had seen any of these things, and they were at once beautiful and heartbreaking. Because they were her mom's.

Billy could see tears welling in her eyes. "Would you like to see what else is here?" he asked. She nodded. Carefully they started picking through the contents of the chest. Each item told a story of two people who apparently shared the good life, not without a sense of tradition and family.

A tablecloth and matching napkins with a Christmas wreathe motif told of festive times. There were graceful lace curtains that were yellowing in plastic bags, probably revered relics from another generation. A pink baby blanket revealed a cow jumping over the moon and bright hopes for the future.

Laura and Billy lifted the contents reverently and placed them, one by one, on a night table. She sighed when she thought she had emptied the chest. A bit suspiciously, Billy tapped the bottom. It sounded hollow. Feeling around, he found a groove, reached in with a finger, and gently lifted the base.

Beneath the false bottom was a mahogany box that was locked shut. Her heart beating rapidly, Laura pulled the gold-plated key out of her pocket and placed it into the lock. The lid opened. Inside the box was a stack of letters in their envelopes, some addressed to Aurora Ames, some to Lorne Bennett. Laura opened one of them.

My darling,

Here I am, 25,000 miles in the sky. It's been only an hour since we kissed and said good-bye, and I miss you already, so much so I want to go back and hold you and never let you go. Screw the movies and the money. I want you ...

It was a letter from her father to her mother before they were married. As she continued reading it, Laura grew more curious but also embarrassed, as if she had stumbled onto someone's private conversation. She stopped reading and put the letter back in its place, then lifted the box of letters out of the chest.

Nearby, Alex was eyeing stacks of cardboard boxes with interest. On one box were the words *Family and Friends* scrolled across it. Inside were photo albums and a large batch of single photos. She leafed through one of the albums and many of the loose photos. A few of the pictures seemed particularly intriguing to her. When she heard her father say, "Come on, Alex. We're ready to go," she closed the box.

Upstairs in the living room, Laura read a couple of letters to herself, then put them back in the box. "I can't read any more of them. Not now," she choked. "They're just so personal and beautiful. I don't know if I have the right."

"Apparently, they loved each other very much," said Billy, "and it's obvious these letters meant a lot to your dad."

Laura nodded, then said, "I'd like to keep them, Aunt Sally."

"I don't see a problem with that," she replied. "Just don't tell your uncle. You know how he is about his stuff."

"I do, but this is not his stuff."

"I guess you're right, darling."

Billy looked over at the sofa, where Alex had fallen asleep.

"Jet lag," Billy surmised.

"I think we better head back to the city," said Laura, hoisting the box of letters under one arm.

PART 6

BEWARE CITY BULLS

25

It was Sunday, the day after the Queens visit. Laura was setting out to do something she had wanted to do for a long time: view the scene of the crime and examine firsthand the place where her mother had been murdered. Accompanied by Billy and Alex, she was both excited and apprehensive about what she would find and how she would react to it.

Police reports offered a graphic description of the murder scene. The victim died at approximately two o'clock in the morning. Death was caused by a single shot to the chest, fired from a .32 caliber handgun at fairly close range, perhaps four or five feet away. No traces of drugs were found in the victim's blood, and there were no marks or signs of a struggle. Except for Lorne Bennett's personal handgun, nothing appeared to be stolen or disturbed.

According to police, the victim was found in the living room of the brownstone apartment she and her husband owned. The trail of blood on the carpet indicated she was trying to crawl to a nearby bedroom where her four-month-old daughter was sleeping. The victim's body was found at about seven o'clock that same morning by a nursemaid. The baby was not hurt, but she was crying when the nursemaid entered the apartment.

On the way to her parents' old apartment, Laura saw someone

she did not expect to see, or want to see. Scotty Brown was walking leisurely toward her on the other side of the street. Laughing and holding hands with a pretty young woman, he seemed just as surprised to see her, and gave her an awkward wave. Laura waved back. Then, after glancing quizzically over at Billy, Scotty put his hand up to his ear, as if to say, "I'll call you," and continued trundling down the block with his dark-haired beauty. Laura shook her head. "Unbelievable."

"Old friend?" asked Billy.

"I guess," Laura replied.

Alex took it up a notch. "Old boyfriend?"

"Yes."

"Men!" Alex concluded.

As difficult as it was, Laura was not about to let a chance meeting with her ex cause her to lose sight of the plan for the day. When they reached the narrow, three-story brownstone, she was struck by the old-town feel and beauty of the neighborhood. It was obviously an expensive and impressive stretch of real estate that residents took pride in keeping that way.

Looking up at the first-floor apartment where her parents had lived, Laura caught sight of an old woman sitting by the window. What a lucky break! Laura made a gesture as if to ask her to open the front door. The woman waved back, a big, warm smile on her face. Laura pointed to the front door once again. This time, the woman nodded that she understood and got up from her chair.

When the entry buzzer sounded, Billy opened the front door and held it open for Laura and Alex. Walking up the elegant, old wooden stairway to the first floor, Laura felt her heart skip a beat. How many times had her mother and father climbed these same steps?

The old woman was waiting in the doorway of her apartment when they arrived at the first-floor landing. She was still smiling. "Yes, what can I do for you?" she asked.

Laura decided to be up-front. "Oh, hi, my name is Laura Bennett and these are my friends, Billy Volpe and his daughter, Alex, and we were wondering whether we could see your apartment. I know that's a silly or odd request, but, you see, I used to live here many years ago, and this apartment meant a lot to me."

"What did you say your name was?"

"Laura Bennett."

"Come on in."

A foyer led to a large, tidy room that Laura surmised must be the place where it happened. Billy held her hand as they entered the room. She fought hard to contain her emotions as her eyes darted everywhere.

"I knew your mother and father," the old woman volunteered. "Very nice people. Kept to themselves but friendly, always willing to lend a hand. Your father sometimes helped me bring my groceries upstairs. I used to live on the top floor when they lived here. When your mother died, God rest her soul, the apartment came up for sale and I moved down here and bought the whole building. My daughter and son-in-law live in the apartments upstairs, separately. Never see much of them. Always on the move, with phones in their ears. Know what I mean?"

Laura nodded. Alex put her hand over her purse, apparently hoping her cell phone would not ring now.

"My husband Oscar passed almost three months ago," the old woman continued. "He was a surgeon, a fine, hardworking man, nervous all the time but you'd never know it. We used to do a lot of entertaining here—nice, friendly parties with a lot of important people—but I don't have many visitors nowadays ... There I go, babbling away. Let me show you around."

Laura looked down at the floor. Gone was the carpeting her mother reportedly dragged herself across as she tried to get to baby Laura's room. In its place was a shiny hardwood floor. "Has the place changed much over the years, I mean, since my parents lived here?" she asked.

"No, not really," the woman replied. "Some new paint here, a little repair there, and, of course, the furnishings are all new."

Laura took a deep breath, then said, "This is the room where my mother was killed, right?"

"Yes, she was found right there where your friend is standing."

Alex moved off the spot.

"You know, people often ask me whether it bothers me to live in a house where someone was murdered," the old woman went on. "No, I tell them. She was a beautiful woman, inside and out; it's comforting to have her spirit—and Oscar's, of course—around me."

"And it's so comforting to hear you say that," said Laura.

"It was incredible, what happened after the news spread about your mother," said the woman. "People from all over the city came to pay their respects. The steps outside and all along the gate were filled with lighted candles and flowers. It was a tribute to how much she was loved."

Laura choked back tears and continued, "Do you remember anything about what happened the night she was murdered?"

"I've been asked that a lot," the woman replied. "Just a couple of weeks ago, a detective, a new detective on the case, asked me the same question."

"Was his name Rios?"

"Yes, that's it. Handsome young man, lovely suit, with the saddest eyes I ever saw. I told him I didn't hear a thing, which was the truth. We were sleeping, and the walls in these old buildings are very thick."

"Did you ever hear Laura's parents fighting?" Billy added.

"You know, that's what that young detective also asked me," the woman replied, "I never heard anything. That doesn't mean they didn't fight, behind closed doors, but they were as sweet as can be whenever I saw them." Then, turning to Laura, she said, "Would you like to see your room?"

Laura took a deep breath, nodded. The three of them followed the woman into what appeared to be a sitting room or den. It contained two leather lounge chairs, an entertainment center, a computer workstation, and two bookcases.

While it was far from a room for an infant now, Laura could only imagine what it looked like when she was a baby. She started tearing up.

"Oh, I'm sorry," said the old woman. "Let me give you a hug."

The last time I saw you, you were just a baby, pretty little thing. I want you to know that Oscar just loved this room."

"It's lovely," said Laura. Then looking toward Billy and Alex, she added, "I think we better go now."

The woman led the three of them to the door. "By the way, my name is Ethel Krinsky," she said. "Come back anytime."

26

Knowing Richie Frisco, even for as short a time as she did, Laura felt that this good man must have been a loving husband, and she felt drawn to his wife, to pay her respects. She and her two friends set out to call on Julie Frisco after visiting the crime scene.

When they arrived at her apartment, they knocked on the door. A young man in a rumpled Army uniform, his tie loosened around his collar, half-opened it.

"Whadayawant?" he huffed.

"Oh, hi, I'm looking for Julie Frisco," Laura replied.

"She's resting. She's not ..."

A woman's voice from somewhere in the dimly lit apartment interrupted him. "Who's there, Tommy?" The sound of slippers could be heard slapping against the tile floor. Then the door was opened the rest of the way, and a large woman in a pink bathrobe appeared.

"Mrs. Frisco? I'm Laura Bennett."

Julie Frisco paused for a moment. Then, flicking on the light, she waved them into the apartment. "Come on in. You have to excuse my son. He just came back from Afghanistan, and with all that's happened here ..."

"I'm so sorry to bother you, Mrs. Frisco," said Laura. "Please accept my condolences. I'd like you to meet my friends Billy Volpe and his daughter, Alex."

Julie skipped the courtesies. "Sit down, all of you. You too, Alex, if you can find a chair." Alex sat on the throw rug in the living room. As she did, a black and white cat jumped on her lap. "That's Penny," explained Julie. "My Richie found her on the roof. No one claimed her, so we kept her." Alex gently petted the cat.

A bit nervously, Laura seized the moment. "I knew your husband only briefly, but I thought of him as my friend. He was a very special person—kind, generous, a real gentleman."

"I know," Julie agreed. "Turn on the kettle, Tommy." When her son left the room, she turned to Laura and said, "He's taking it real hard. They were very close. When my Richie came out of prison, he spent a lot of time with the boy. You know, making up for lost time."

Laura nodded.

"Yeah, well," Julie continued, "after my Richie died, some people asked me, How can you be so strong after such a terrible thing? You know what I told them? I told them I'm a survivor. I learned a long time ago, even before my breast cancer, you have to keep on going. What's the point of cursing God for every bad thing that happens to you and tearing your hair out? My Richie used to say to me, 'Worrying is like doing time for a crime you didn't commit.' "

Tommy walked back into the living room, a bottle of beer in his hand, and flopped down on the armchair.

Julie turned to Laura and said, "My husband always spoke highly of you. He really wanted to help you. As I think you know, he loved your father and would do anything for him. When my Richie was in jail, your father helped us get through some difficult times. Just like he did for you."

"What do you mean?" asked Laura.

"Don't you know?"

"All I know is that he took off when I was an infant and left me with my aunt and uncle," said Laura.

Julie drew in a deep breath. "He did what he thought he had to do at the time, but he never, ever, wanted to hurt you, and he never, ever, forgot you," she continued. "Even before he fled, he set up a fund through Richie to take care of whatever you needed ... money for your clothes, your doctors, your education ... for birthdays, holidays, even your first apartment."

Laura was dumbfounded by what she had just heard. "I didn't know," she murmured, terrible hurt and pain in her eyes.

"Now you do, honey."

"No one ever told me," Laura added."Why would my aunt and uncle keep that information from me?"

"Maybe they didn't think you needed to know," Julie offered.

Anger rose like fire in Laura's eyes now. "What else haven't they told me?"

Julie shrugged. "The thing to keep in mind is that your father loved you very much and never, never forgot you."

Fighting back tears, Laura said, "If he loved me so much, why did he run away?"

"What, and be put away for life for something he didn't do?"

"How do you know he didn't do it?"

"I don't know for sure," Julie replied, "but I know your father. I don't think he would ever do anything like that? There was one thing his Aunt Rose used to drill into him: Take the high road; there's more to see up there."

Julie continued, "I know my Richie felt the same way about Lorney as I do, and he was working hard to see if he could clear your father's name."

"Please, Mrs. Frisco, tell us what your husband knew. Everything," Laura pleaded.

"You probably know as much as I do," said Julie. After a pause, she added, "I know my Richie had his eye on a guy from the neighborhood called Reggie Lacey. He was just released from prison. Bad news. But he may have information about what happened that night."

"Any relation to Ned Lacey?" asked Billy.

"Brothers. But there's no great love between them," Julie replied.

"Maybe we should pay a visit to Reggie Lacey," Laura said.

"If you do, better be careful," Julie emphasized. "He's a man with his back against the wall. One more big conviction, and they throw away the keys on him."

The tea pot started whistling. "Would you shut that off, Tommy?" said Julie. "Let's have some tea. Milk, Alex?"

"I like tea," said the girl.

27

They found Reggie Lacey in the backyard of an old apartment on Eleventh Avenue. A squat man with a tightly wound body built up in the prison system, he was sunning himself among the weeds in a dilapidated lawn chair. He had a can of beer in one hand and a cigar in the other.

After introducing herself as Lorne Bennett's daughter, Laura eased into conversation with Reggie, but it was clear she was moving into an area he didn't want to enter.

"What do you know about Richie Frisco's death?" Laura finally asked, straight out.

"Look, whadayawant from me?" Reggie snapped back. "I just got out of the joint, and I ain't plannin' to go back. I don't know nothin', okay?"

"Don't you think you owe it to him, to my father?" she pressed.

"Hey, I'd like to help Lorney's girl," he replied, "but like I said, I don't need no more trouble." He sniffed, wriggled in his chair, then took a gulp of beer.

Alex sat down on a nearby bench and cupped her head in her hands. "If you don't mind me saying, Mr. Lacey," she said, "I think you know something."

Reggie sat up straight. "HEY, WHO THE HELL ARE YOU?"

"Easy, that's my daughter, and you don't have to shout," said Billy. "And you know what? I think she's right."

Reggie stared at the girl, then brushed her off with the palm of his hand. "Ah, what the hell does she know?"

"Look, Mr. Lacey," said Laura. "I think you owe it to Richie to tell us what you know. After all, he did a lot for you and the other guys in prison."

"Suppose so," he mumbled.

"Presents for the kids and grandkids at Christmas," she continued. "Phone calls and letters to attorneys. Doctor bills. Even making rent payments."

"And who do you think helped Richie over the years?" Billy quickly added.

"Mr. Bennett," Alex offered.

Reggie, the divorced father of two children he hardly knew, gave her a sideways glance. Then, turning to Laura, he said, "Why should I tell you anything?"

"Maybe because it's the right thing to do," Billy suggested.

Reggie laughed falsely, rose from his chair, and turned to Billy. "You got some nerve tellin' me what's right," he said. "Where're you from, anyway?"

"Originally, the Bronx," Billy boasted.

"You don't sound like no Bronx person I know," Reggie blurted. He headed for the backyard door.

"Wait," Laura pleaded. He stopped. "I'm not looking to get you in trouble. I'm just looking for a little information."

Reggie sighed. "I don't get it. What's Richie's death have to do with you?"

"He was my friend," Laura replied. "He was trying to help me find out what really happened the night my mother was murdered, whether or not my father was involved. I believe he was close to telling me something when he was pushed off the roof."

"PUSHED?" His face reddened.

"Yes, pushed," Laura continued. "Don't you see? Whoever killed him thought he was getting too close to the truth, and ...."

"Sorry, can't help you," Reggie interrupted.

Laura persisted. "One more thing: What does your brother have to do with any of this?"

"What my brother does is his business," he fumed, heaving his beer can across the yard. "The less I know about his business, the better." He snuffed out the stub of his cigar with his boot and stormed into the house.

It was turning dark when Laura and her friends got back to the hotel. During a light dinner in the café, they quietly reviewed the events of the day, and they all agreed that Reggie was covering up something. While they didn't have to say it, they also knew they were wading into dangerous waters by questioning him about events he obviously didn't want to talk about. Laura was especially struck by how angry Reggie became when the conversation turned to his brother, Ned.

After dinner, they went up to the room, where Laura and Billy shared some pinot noir and discussed their next move. Clearly, Ned Lacey was a person of interest, to use the language of law enforcement. Atop one of the beds, Alex nodded in agreement, yawned, and fell asleep.

The room went silent. Laura rose from her chair, walked over to the window, and gazed at a city's changing into night. Billy got up and stood next to her. She seemed sad.

"Spectacular, isn't it?" he said, gesturing toward the view below.

She nodded, a half-hearted smile on her face.

"Thinking about your old friend, the one we saw today?" he asked.

"No, of course not ... Well, maybe, yes, a little," she said. "We were so close. We were even talking about getting married someday, and raising a family, as soon as we were more settled in our careers. He wanted to open his own business, and I promised to help him.

"I mean, we just broke up," she continued. "He hated that I was spending so much time trying to find out about my mother and father, and what happened that night."

"I don't understand that, Laura."

"You wouldn't, Billy. You and Alex just traveled across country to help me." Then quietly, but angrily, she added, "Better I find out about him now than later."

"Want me to break his legs?" Billy asked.

She wondered whether he was serious, but only for a moment. They both laughed.

"Ah, that's better," he said. Reaching over to touch her cheek, he added, "You have beautiful eyes when you laugh, Laura."

"Thanks. You do, too, Billy." It was as if they were looking at each other for the first time. They embraced, kissed.

She smiled "Whew!" She glanced over at the bed where Alex was sleeping. "I think I'd better go."

"I'll ride down with you."

"No, please. I'll just grab a cab out front. Talk to you tomorrow."

It was a long, remarkable day. Laura was reflective as she jumped into a cab and headed home in the darkened streets. As she got out of the taxi and walked to the front entrance, she had a feeling someone was watching her from across the street. She turned, thought she saw someone in the shadows, but continued into the lobby.

28

LAURA LAY IN BED SEARCHING FOR ANSWERS to many unanswered questions. She wondered whether it was a good idea, emotionally, to have visited the apartment where her mother was murdered. Did she really think that Scotty wouldn't find a new companion right away? How is it that she wasn't informed that her father was sending money to her aunt and uncle for her? It was only a kiss, but could that moment of intimacy with Billy be the start of something wonderful, a new kind of relationship between equals, or will it end nowhere again, with a wave from across the street?

The sun was starting to seep through the lace curtains when she finally dozed off. She didn't know how long she was sleeping when something startled her. Laura lunged for the phone. "Hello," she rasped, unprepared for the day's first challenge. When she heard who was calling, she sat up on the side of the bed. "Oh, hi, Detective, I was going to call you."

"Hi, Ms. Bennett, what's happening?" Rios asked.

Laura fell short of telling him everything, but she did report on the meeting with Reggie

Lacey. "He knows something, I just know it," she tried to persuade him. "Can't you guys bring him into the station house and question him?"

"On what grounds?" asked Rios coolly.

"I don't know, maybe on suspicion he knows something."

"About what?"

"The murder of Richie, maybe even something about my mother's murder."

"What makes you think Richie Frisco was murdered?"

"Instinct ... gut feeling."

"We need more than instinct or gut feeling. Now I'm not saying Richie wasn't pushed, but I don't think Reggie can tell us anything. All he wants to do, according to our sources, is get as far away from here as possible with his girlfriend. The last thing he wants is trouble. One more felony would land him back in prison for good."

"And what about his brother Ned?"

"Ned has an alibi that seems to hold up now. He was at a boxing match at the Garden the night Richie fell—or was pushed—to his death."

A curtain of silence descended between them.

"Do yourself a big favor, Ms. Bennett," Rios warned her. "Stop being a cop. You're playing with fire, and you can get burned, real bad. You and your two friends."

"How do you know about them?"

"We know."

"They're friends of mine from Arizona," she explained. "I was just showing them around town."

"There are lots of places to see in New York besides the West Side."

When she hung up, Laura fell back on the soft, cool sheets and closed her eyes. She tried to go back to sleep, but couldn't. Something kept prodding her to get up. Finally, she glanced at the clock, blurted out an obscenity, and shot out of bed. As she pulled clothes out of the closet, she picked up the phone and called her office to say she would be late. With remarkable dexterity, she managed to get dressed in fifteen minutes.

As she dashed out the front door of the building, Laura spotted an empty cab cruising up the street, hailed it and hopped into the back seat. After telling the driver where she wanted to go, she phoned Anita, who was already at her desk.

"Where the hell are you?" said Anita. "I walked by your office twice."

"I'm on my way, but first I have to make a stop," Laura explained. Then, one eye on the cabbie through the rear view mirror, she asked in a whisper whether she had received any more threats by "The Hound of Hell" or anyone else.

"No, but you better ... I mean, I don't know how to make this clearer. There's a nut job out there with an attitude, and you're pissing him off."

"I know, I know."

"Aren't you scared?"

"Of course. I've never been more frightened in my life."

"So, why don't you back off? At least for awhile," said Anita. "Why not let that detective what's his name see what he can do?"

"Rios."

"Yeah. Why not give him a chance?"

"We talk when we can, Rios and I, and we share information. I wish I could say he's making progress, Anita, but I don't think he is."

"And I suppose you are."

"Yes. Well, maybe." Laura rehashed her meeting with Reggie. "I think he's hiding something. So does Billy."

"Billy?"

Laura went on to tell her about Billy and Alex and their encounters with her father. "They came here from Arizona to tell me about him," she said. "Now they want to help me clear his name, if that's possible."

"That's nice," said Anita, clear skepticism in her voice.

"Trust me," Laura snapped back. "They're good people. You'd like them."

"Okay, okay, but what makes you think Reggie is hiding anything?"

"Something in his voice, the way he acted, reacted," Laura whispered. "Here's what I think: Richie was getting too close to finding out what happened that night when someone pushed him."

"Who?"

"I don't know, but I think Reggie knows."

Anita took a deep breath, apparently trying to digest it all. "I can't keep up with you."

"Something else," Laura continued, her eyes darting toward the cab driver again.

"There's something else?" said Anita.

Laura then told her about the money she had been receiving over the years through Richie.

"So, what does that mean?" asked Anita.

"It means there are things about my father I never knew. For one thing, he cared for me more than I ever imagined."

"That's good, right?"

"Yeah, but I don't understand why I never knew what he did for me," said Laura, raising her voice. "Why didn't Aunt Sally and Uncle Roger tell me?"

Anita searched for an answer, then said, "Maybe your father just didn't want you to know."

"Maybe," Laura sighed.

"Listen, is there anything I can do?" Anita added.

"Yes. Do me a favor: Drop in on my aunt and uncle and see if they're alright. I don't want to scare them, but maybe you can find out if they've received any threats."

The cabdriver turned slightly to hear better.

"Sure," said Anita. "Where're you headed now?"

"I've got to make one stop, on the West Side."

"Ah, come on, Miss Marple! Come on in now. We need you here."

"This won't take long," said Laura.

"Look, if you need any help, give me a call. I mean it!" said Anita. "I'll call my uncle Sal and his son, the one with the Bow-Flex."

29

WHEN SHE FINALLY SUMMONED THE RESOLVE, Laura entered the West Side Demolition Company's offices, which occupied the ground floor of a tenement relic on Eleventh Avenue. Walking down a corridor, Laura came to a long room containing a wall of multi-colored file cabinets and a sagging gray sofa and two soiled easy chairs that probably once matched. Laura surmised that this was the waiting room.

Behind an old, oak desk sat a gray-haired woman chatting on the phone, her back to the door. Laura decided not to announce herself and kept walking until she came to the next office. This time the door was closed. Laura knocked twice.

"Come in," barked someone on the other side.

Laura slowly opened the door and walked into the room.

"Yes?" said a short, muscular man behind a gray metal desk.

"Ned Lacey?" she asked

"Yeah."

Something about him looked familiar. Then it dawned on her. He was the man that opened the taxi door for her the morning she met Richie in the diner.

"My name is Laura Bennett."

"I know who you are," he said. The veins in his neck became visible, and the man drew a long, deep breath. His hands folded behind his head, he leaned back in his chair. "Well, well, Lorney Bennett's daughter?"

"Yes."

"What can I do for you?"

She was trembling, and her heart, pounding. Laura slid into a chair without being asked. "I need some information, and I think you can help me, Mr. Lacey," she began. He shifted his weight. "It's about Richie Frisco, a good friend of mine. There's a ..."

"A sweetheart! It's a shame what happened to him," he broke in. "As many times as he went onto the roof, he just got careless one day, slipped, and fell, poor guy."

"There's a rumor he didn't fall," she said. "There's a rumor he was pushed."

"Nah, Nah, he fell, he fell," he insisted. "Who's going to push good old Richie?"

"I don't know. I was hoping you had some ideas," she said.

His eyes narrowed. "How would I know?"

"You have a lot of connections around the neighborhood," she replied. "You know a lot."

"Nah, trust me. Like I said, he fell," he said with finality. "How else can I help you?"

She took a deep breath. "Did you know my father?"

Lacey exploded in laughter. "Are you kidding? Everybody in the neighborhood knew Lorney, and everyone loved him. He had a lot of fans on the West Side, including my wife. She used to go out with him, that is, before I met her. When Lorney became a big star in Hollywood, everyone idolized him and wanted to share in his success."

"What do you mean?"

"You know, local boy makes good. Everyone wants a piece of the action. It's just human nature, right?"

Laura didn't answer. "What do you know about the night my mother was killed? Do you have any idea who murdered my mom? Do you have any idea where my father was?"

"Whoa, whoa," said Lacey. "Look, kid, save yourself a lot of heartache. It was all over the papers. Your father and mother were having big-time marital problems, and he was still mad as hell when he stormed up to their apartment, after a heavy night of drinking, and shot her dead. End of story."

"I don't think so," Laura went on, summoning more courage. "It doesn't add up. That's not my father."

"How would you know?" he sneered. "You were only a baby."

"Yeah, I know," she replied. "I was asleep in the next room when my mother was shot, remember?" She decided to take a stab in the dark. "It doesn't add up because it's not what Richie told me."

Lacey jumped up out of his chair, the veins bulging in his sweaty forehead. "Richie's a rotten, stinking liar," he shouted as he slid around the desk and stood over her, his nostrils flared out in rage. Laura got up, fearing she was about to be gored by the angry bull in front of her. He stared up at her with furious and loathing eyes.

Unexpectedly, his receptionist appeared in the doorway. "Oh," said Gracie, "I didn't know you had anyone back here with you. A pained look on her face, she dropped some mail on his desk and backed out of the room.

"Oh, I was just leaving," said Laura, seizing the opportunity.

Lacey said nothing as Laura brushed past the receptionist and walked down the long corridor and out the front door.

When she got outside, Laura heaved a sigh of relief and headed for her office.

As she was about to enter the building where she worked, she brushed into a tall man in sunglasses with a slightly weathered face. He had on jeans, a long-sleeved shirt, and a worn cowboy hat. Laura thought he looked familiar. The man seemed surprised by the unexpected encounter. "Excuse me," he said, almost under his breath. Then he smiled, looked at his watch, and walked away. Laura followed him for a moment before making a dash for the lobby.

30

It was just Laura's luck she'd run into the creative director as she entered the building. Cheerful and talkative on most mornings, Sumner Grady seemed glum and tense today. Laura expected the worst when he stopped and gently guided her away from everyone.

"Listen, Laura," he said, "I'm on the run. Got to see a nervous client. Let me see what you have on that new teen cosmetics line when I get back this afternoon."

"Sure," she gulped, as she thanked her workplace angel for helping her dodge the bullet one more time.

Once she got to her desk, Laura went right to work and kept at it all day. She hardly had time to answer her phone or e-mail messages, but she couldn't ignore them. Late in the afternoon, when the phone rang, she snapped it up after one ring, but no one appeared to be on the other end. She hung up. The phone rang again. It was Billy.

"WAS THAT YOU?" she exploded.

"Was that me what?" he said.

"Never mind," she said more calmly. "Just a little bit on edge today."

"I just want you to know I really enjoyed last night. I hope you did, too."

"Yes, I did," she said, slightly embarrassed. "What's up?"

"We need to see you."

"Is it urgent?"

"It could be," he replied.

"Well, I have some ad copy that needs tweaking, along with a couple of meetings," she said. "If it's alright with you, let's meet in that little Greek restaurant by my apartment. Six-thirty, okay?"

"Okay."

It was earlier than usual when Ned Lacey got home. Glancing at his wife Frances, who was sitting by the window, he mumbled a greeting and headed straight for the bedroom. He couldn't reach his brother that day, as he had hoped to do; nor was there time to go look for him now. He pulled out a large overnight bag and began packing.

"Frances, where're all my underwear?" he shouted.

"In the laundry basket in the kitchen," she answered. "They're all clean and folded."

He walked by her and headed for the kitchen.

"What are you doing?" she asked.

He stopped. "Packing. I'm leaving," he barked, as if she should have known.

"Why?"

"I've got to go," he grumbled. "There are rumblings out there, from people I know in the right places. Things are getting too hot for me around here. You must have figured that would happen someday."

"Don't you think it's time you stopped trying to make everyone believe you don't know what happened that night?"

"And go to jail?"

She took her time before saying it. "If that's what you have to do ..."

He couldn't believe what she had just said. "Don't forget, you're in this, too, Frances. Are you ready to go to prison?"

"All I know is I want some peace, and not the constant worry that someone's going to come in the middle of the night and haul us both away."

"I got to go now," said Ned.

"And what do I do while you're gone?" she cried out.

"You can sit by the window and wait for your son to come down the street, like you always do. I can't afford to stay here, and it's better I go alone."

"I don't want you to go, Ned."

He took a deep breath and tried to exhale all of his anger, fears, and frustration. "Look, this might all blow over in a couple of days. I'll call you as soon as I can. Come here, give us a kiss." She did, and he kissed her back, holding on to a thread of tender feelings for the only one that meant anything to him in his life.

"Don't say anything to anyone," he told her. "Remember, we're both involved in this, and you don't want Robby to come back to an empty house."

After completing his packing, he looked around, wondering whether he would ever see his home or his wife again, and left.

At the restaurant, Laura noticed that Billy and Alex seemed subdued as they all began eating. She tried to set a more cheerful tone. "So what did you do today?"

Billy took a bite of his sandwich. "Nothing much."

"Let's see," Alex added, sipping her hot tea with lemon.

"Don't you feel well, Alex?" Laura asked, glancing at her drink.

"No, I just like tea with lemon," she explained. Then, in a sing-song voice, she said, "First, we went to the Empire State Building, then lunch in Little Italy, then a boat trip to Ellis Island, then another boat ride, this time to the Statue of Liberty. My dad wants to go up to his old neighborhood in the Bronx tomorrow. We're going to rent a car."

"You guys must be exhausted," Laura observed, stabbing a tomato in her salad.

They both nodded, lacking any enthusiasm in their faces.

Laura stopped eating. "Okay, what's going on?" she asked.

Alex wiped her mouth with a napkin and reached into the handbag with the shoulder strap and pulled out some photographs. As Alex handed them to Laura, Billy said, "We hesitated to show these to you. Alex found them in the basement with your parents' things. We're not sure what they mean, but we think you should see them and draw your own conclusions."

The first photograph Laura picked up was actually a sleeve of pictures, probably taken at an arcade. It showed Roger Kent and Aurora, probably in their late teens or early twenties, in various romantic poses. "Look at the back," Billy gently urged her. The words "OUR FIRST DATE" seemed to surprise Laura. "I didn't know," she began. Equally revealing were the other photographs—the couple looking lovingly into each other's eyes, cuddled up on a couch, kissing on a boat ride.

"I didn't have a clue," said Laura absently. "I guess that's one more secret I should have known." She sat in stony silence. *How is it that Uncle Roger once carried on a romance with my mother, and I never knew about it? Did Aunt Sally know and, if she did, how did she take it? Did my father know? When did it occur, and ...*

"I hope you're not upset," said Billy.

"Why should I be?" she said, unable to hide the storm brewing just beneath the surface. "If you don't mind, I'll keep these."

"Sure," said Billy.

"We just wanted to help you," said Alex.

"Yes, I know," said Laura as she excused herself to go to the ladies room.

Laura preferred to walk home alone from the restaurant. As she neared the front door, she saw a familiar figure. Detective Rios was dialing someone on his cell phone. He aborted the call when he saw Laura and walked up to her.

"What's going on?" she asked.

"A couple of new developments you should know about," he replied. "Ned Lacey is nowhere to be found. He's gone ... vanished. We paid a visit to his home, to bring him in for questioning. His wife said he left, she didn't know where he went, and she didn't know when he'd be back. Is there anything, anything at all, he said when you visited him that might help us find him?"

Laura was surprised he knew she had visited Ned Lacey, but she decided to answer his question anyway. "No, not really," she replied. "He seemed a little testy, guarded. I think he knows something." Shaking her head in disbelief, she said, "Just one more thing, Detective: How come you know so much about me and my whereabouts and so little about guys like Ned Lacey?"

He sighed. "We've been all over the neighborhood, day and night, since Richie's death. Up to now, we really didn't have reason to talk to Ned Lacey. But that's changed. Two people, teenagers, said they saw him on the roof the day Richie fell or was pushed. That's why we went to see him."

It was a major turn of events, and Laura was encouraged by it, but she didn't feel like cheering, not tonight. "And have you talked to Ned's brother?" she added.

"We can't find Reggie, either. We have a few questions for him, too."

Laura's cell phone rang. "Let me call you back," she whispered to the caller.

"You alright?" Anita asked.

"I'm fine," Laura muttered.

"You don't sound it. Want me to come over?"

"Absolutely not! It's late."

"Oh," Anita added, "I dropped in to see your aunt and uncle. As far as I can tell, they're good. We had a nice chat. Talked about nest eggs and healthcare coverage and all the stuff you talk about when you're getting ready to retire, but they didn't once mention threats."

"That's great. Call you later, alright?" After she hung up, Laura turned to Rios and said, "I have to go. I'll keep what you told me in mind."

"I hope I didn't upset you, but I thought you should know what's going on, for your own safety. Call me if you have any questions or if you just feel like talking," he added.

She nodded and walked toward the front door. Standing at the curb, Charlie, the doorman, waved when she saw her. Next to him was a tall man in a cowboy hat, his face partially hidden by the way he was standing. Both men were holding coffee containers in their hands. Laura waved back and headed for the elevator. Once again, she was not in the mood for casual conversation.

Crossing the George Washington Bridge, Ned Lacey felt the anger building inside him. Sooner or later, his temper always got the better of him, and he'd obsess over what he should have or should not have done. This evening, he was berating himself for not taking better aim at Lorney's girl when he tossed the scaffolding down on her that morning. He should have finished the job, instead of merely trying to scare her, and the late-night calls were also a waste.

By the time he crossed the bridge, Ned had worked himself into an almost uncontrollable rage. He screeched off the highway onto the nearest exit and made a U-turn back to the city, but he would not go home. Laura had to be dealt with first. She'd have to pay the ultimate price, while—once again—he wouldn't have to pay a dime, so he thought.

PART 7

SAVE THE BUTTERFLY

31

LAURA AWOKE EARLY THE FOLLOWING DAY, TOO early. Drained by another restless night, she nevertheless decided to get up and prepare for work. She had often marveled at the human psyche. How can anyone manage to be bright and creative during life's darker, more anxious moments? But she had done it before; she would do it again.

It was a beautiful morning with a gentle breeze from the Northwest as she left home. She decided to walk to work through Central Park, as she had done before when she had a lot on her mind. Perhaps a walk in the park would clear up some of the confusion and give her a new perspective.

Except for a runner here and a walker there and an occasional cyclist, Laura did not see anyone along the path she took. She was enjoying the landscape and the rhythmic chirping of hungry birds. Everywhere there were butterflies—probably the last butterflies of summer—and Laura, a nature lover, stopped for a moment and watched them in flight and at rest. Struck by their innocence, beauty, and vulnerability, she wondered what life would be without those precious creatures.

Deeper into the park, she began to sense that someone was following her. Given the dangers that she faced lately, it was a normal reaction, she told herself. *Calm down; you're just a little jumpy*. However, as she neared a tunnel under a bridge arched lovingly over a hilly but picturesque patch of earth, she took a firmer grip on her handbag strap. *Nothing is going to happen, nothing is going to happen.*

Midway through the tunnel she saw someone moving toward her. Laura strained to get a clearer view, but the person was lost in the morning light. She tried to shadow her eyes from the sun. Suddenly, she stopped as the figure, a man in plaid shorts, extended his arm high in the air and waved. "Good morning," said the walker. She just managed a return a greeting and headed out of the tunnel, relieved but shaking.

Entering another seemingly desolate part of the park, Laura again felt uneasy and picked up her pace. Reaching into her bag, she pulled out her cell phone and dialed Anita for a little company and conversation along the way. But before she could finish dialing, she heard this frantic breathing and rustling behind her. She turned, and this stocky man came charging out of a row of bushes like a wild bull and slammed her to the ground, sending her cell phone flying into the surrounding thicket.

When she started to scream, the man leapt on top of her and covered her mouth with one of his thick, powerful hands. With the other, he drew a knife out of his back pocket and held it to the side of her neck. "Shut up! Shut up, you bitch!" he growled. Laura stopping screaming and stared up at her attacker.

She was shocked and terrified as she recognized Ned Lacey, a crazed look in his bloodshot eyes, straddling her. He slowly withdrew his hand from her mouth. Laura took some quick, deep breaths but she dared not scream. "What do you want?" she stuttered.

"You!" he spat out. "If it weren't for you ... Why couldn't you mind your own business? You and your friend, Richie Frisco. Well, it's over, OVER! What I know about what happened twenty-two years ago, you'll never know."

Laura stared up at Lacey, incredulous, stunned by what he had just told her. *He knows something, he knows something!*

"It all stops now," Lacey gloated. "Take a good look at a 'mugger' who's going to stab you and take your purse."

Laura tried to twist her body out of his vise-like grip, but she couldn't.

"What, you don't like my plan?" he snarled.

She screamed, and once again he clamped his hand over her mouth. She tried to bite him, but it was useless. His hand was as tough as old harness leather.

"I waited and waited for you to come out all morning," he went on, a wild look in his eyes. "I didn't know how I was going to do it, but then ..." He let out a fiendish laugh. "You decided to walk to work through the park. Lucky me!"

Laura managed to pull away from his hand and shrieked. Lacey covered her mouth again with one hand; with the other, he angled the knife to the side of her throat. As she tried to wriggle away, this figure came storming down the path, yanked Lacey off of her, and flung him to the ground. Kicking the knife away, the stranger jumped on Lacey and began punching him. Lacey broke loose and, after struggling to his feet, rammed into the stranger and knocked him down. Lacey jumped on top of him and slammed the side of the man's face into the ground. The stranger twisted out of his grip and began trading blows with Lacey. Suddenly, he grabbed Lacey by the back of his neck and flung him into the bushes. When the stranger bent over Lacey and started pummeling him with both hands, Laura shouted, "Please, please, that's enough!"

Lacey lay unconscious. The stranger got up and dusted himself off. Trying to catch his breath, he pointed to a cowboy hat that lay nearby and said, "Excuse me, I've got to get my hat."

"WHO ARE YOU?" she demanded.

"Nobody," he replied, as he bent over to retrieve his hat. "Just a stranger who happened to be in the right place at the right time."

By this time, several people, including a police officer, had heard her screams and came running over to her. "Are you alright, lady?" "What's going on?" "Who did this to you?" As Laura, shaking, tried to explain what had happened, she looked down the path for the stranger who had saved her life. He was gone.

Police and EMS tried to persuade Laura to go to the emergency room, but she insisted she was fine, more shaken than hurt. More than anything else, she just wanted some space, some time alone.

Just the thought of it made her shudder: A knife was about to be plunged into her! Were it not for the stranger with the cowboy hat she would be dead now! She just had to get away, to a safe place. She wanted to go home.

32

A̲t a hastily called meeting of the cold
case unit, Detective Rios announced that the Aurora Bennett
murder case was "on the verge of breaking wide open." He began
by reminding everyone that Richie Frisco had been helping Laura
Bennett obtain information about her parents—and some of that
information raised suspicions about Ned Lacey.

"Correct? Then what happens," he continued. "Frisco falls
five stories, from the roof of his apartment building, to his death.
Coincidence? Yesterday morning, two teenagers come forward
and say they saw Ned Lacey on the roof that day. Does that mean
that Frisco was pushed and did not accidentally fall or jump?
Maybe.

"It gets better," he went on "Yesterday afternoon, when we go
over to Lacey's house to pick him up for questioning, he is gone.
Vanished. And his wife doesn't know where he went." Rios took a
deep breath. "On top of that, just a little while ago, we get word
that Lacey was arrested this morning for attacking Laura Bennett
with a knife in Central Park while she was on her way to work."

There was a hush in the room. Then, one by one, they called
for a new review of the evidence in the case, particularly as it
related to Lacey.

Detective Rennie Halsey urged caution. "It looks open and

shut on what this guy did to Laura Bennett in the park, but we still don't have much to go on when it comes to Aurora Bennett's murder," he argued.

"That's why we need to take a hard look at this thing," Detective Rachel Levine quickly added.

"No question about it," said Detective Denny Esposito. "Lacey's one slippery guy, but how could he have slipped through the cracks all these years?"

"Let's find out," said Rios. "First things first. We go down and talk to this guy."

Outside the Bronx apartment building where he had lived as a small boy, Billy Volpe took his phone out of his shirt pocket and tried calling Laura again. No one answered, and Billy didn't leave a message this time, as he had done twice before. "Any luck?" asked Alex as she sipped some orange juice.

Billy shook his head, a worried look in his usually playful eyes. "I've called her cell, I've called her home, I've called her office. Nothing! Where the hell is she?"

Alex shook her head, as concerned as her father.

"She seemed a little upset and angry when we left her last night," said Billy. "Maybe we shouldn't have showed her those photos."

"Maybe we should call Detective Rios," Alex suggested.

Billy hesitated. "I don't know. I don't think so. But I've had enough sightseeing for today."

"Let's just go back to the hotel, dad, and try reaching her there."

Anita was beside herself when Laura failed to show up for work without notifying the office. Looking back at it, she thought Laura was not too talkative the night before. *Something was bothering her.* Anita was sorry she didn't go to her apartment when she offered to do so.

She tried calling Laura herself. When that didn't work, Anita flipped through Laura's Rolodex for some cell numbers and started making calls.

Billy Volpe said he had been frantically trying to reach Laura himself. I'll keep trying."

"Me, too. Let me know if you hear anything," she said.

Anita also called Uncle Roger. There was no answer at first, and she left a message. When he called back and heard that Laura couldn't be reached, he sounded worried and said he'd do some checking around. Asked whether he thought his wife might know where Laura was, he said he didn't think so. "I just talked to her. She didn't say anything. She was on her way to a church meeting."

Anita even contacted Scotty Brown, who seemed mildly concerned. "I bumped into her on the street a few days ago, but I haven't seen her since," he said. "Ask her to call me when she has a chance." Anita had a couple of words for him, but she didn't want to complicate things; she said nothing.

When Detectives Rios and Levine arrived at the station house where they were holding Ned Lacey, they didn't recognize the man. Gone was the cocky neighborhood big shot they had been observing for the past several weeks.

Lacey, bruised and battered, was slumped in a worn-out chair, apparently trying to sleep after the beating he took from the stranger in the park. When Rios and Levine entered the room, he jumped up and started shouting, "WHERE THE HELL IS HE? I WANT MY LAWYER ... NOW! His fleshy face was pale and sweaty, and his eyes were filled with terror. His ripped, dirty shirt and matching pants were a sharp contrast to the well-tailored clothes in front of him.

"Calm down, Ned. You know your rights," said Rios.

Lacey sat down. "I need to talk to my wife, too," he said, restored to some degree of sanity. He brushed down his messy, thinning hair with the palm of his hand.

"No problem," said Levine. "We just want to have a little talk with you."

"Whatever that bitch said is bullshit," thundered Lacey as he bolted out of the chair. "She was asking for it. She's been hounding me and spreading lies about me. Was I angry? Sure. Was I going to kill her? Of course not. Me? Ned Lacey?"

"There's a lot of hard evidence against you, but that's not what we want to talk with you about," said Rios.

Lacey's face was twitching now. He sat back down.

"We now have good reason to believe Richie Frisco was pushed off the roof that evening," Rios began.

"Nah! Richie fell, Richie fell," Ned insisted.

"We know you were worried that Richie was feeding information about you to Lorne Bennett's daughter, information you didn't want to come out," Rios continued.

"THAT'S CRAZY!"

"We now have two witnesses who said they saw you on the roof the nigh Richie was there," he reported.

"WHAT? THAT'S A LIE! I was at a boxing match. You know that. "

"They swore."

"No way, no way!"

"After what happened this morning, who's going to believe you?" said Levine.

"It wasn't me."

"Then who?" she asked.

"I don't know. I don't know."

"They were sure," Levine pressed.

"It had to be someone else. Maybe, my brother. Yeah, it was probably my brother. He looks just like me, and ... " Lacey stopped. "Like I said, I want my lawyer."

Rios' cell phone rang. He pulled it out of his pocket, gave a quick hello, and just listened. When the caller finished talking, he said, "Okay, okay. We'll be right there."

Levine knew it was time to leave. Getting up from her chair, she said, "We'll talk some more soon, Ned." Rios nodded in agreement.

"Yeah, right," said Lacey.

"What's going on?" asked Levine once they got outside.

"They picked up Reggie Lacey," Rios explained. "He was boarding a bus for Denver with his girlfriend. Let's go see what he has to say."

Detective Rios went right to the point when they saw Reggie. "We just had a nice chat with your brother. He was arrested this morning. Attempted assault with a deadly weapon. Attempted murder. And a couple of other things."

"So?" said Reggie. "What does that have to do with me?"

"You might be interested to know that he was arrested for trying to kill Laura Bennett, a good friend of Richie Frisco's," Rios explained.

Reggie started squirming in his chair. "Yeah? So?"

"We have good reason to believe now that Richie was pushed from the roof that evening," Rios continued. "Your brother is connecting you with Richie's murder."

"WHAT?" said Reggie. "He's nuts."

"We have two witnesses, swore they saw your brother on the roof that evening," Rios continued. "Your brother says that was you, not him. He said he was at a boxing match, which seems to hold up."

"Once again, the bastard's trying to worm himself out of trouble," Reggie exploded.

"What were you and Milly doing on the bus this morning?" Levine jumped in.

"Why, is it against the law to take a bus trip with a girl?" Reggie replied.

"To Denver?" asked Levine.

"It was an emergency."

"Let me see," she noted. "You were going to Denver, without telling your parole board?"

"I was going to tell," Reggie muttered.

"Excuse me, I can hardly hear you," said Levine.

"I said I was going to tell my parole board."

"Were you also going to tell them about the $15,000 in your pocket?" she asked.

Reggie took a deep breath. "Got a smoke?" Both detectives shook their heads. Reggie, disappointed, closed his eyes, as if it were all a bad dream. "Can we talk?" he asked.

After Laura returned home from the park, she gathered up the photos that Billy and Alex had given her and spread them on the dining room table. One by one, she picked them up and examined them under the overhead chandelier. She still couldn't believe that her mother and Uncle Roger were once so close. How could she not have known? She searched among her memories. One scene flashed by ...

Laura was about six or seven, and she was in a car with Uncle Roger. "Where're we going?" she asked.

"It's a surprise," he said.

When they got to the cemetery, he drove to the far end and stopped.

"Do you know what today is?" he asked as he got out of car.

Laura shook her head.

"It's your mother's birthday, and we're going to pay her a visit."

This was the first time she was at her mother's gravesite. Uncle Roger brought out a small azalea plant from the car trunk and started planting it. Laura helped with her little shovel.

"It's the least we can do," he said, tears welling in his eyes.

On the way home, Uncle Roger asked Laura to promise not to tell Aunt Sally about their little secret visit to the cemetery. "I don't want to upset her."

Laura promised.

Back in her apartment, she lay down to rest, but the phone kept ringing. Finally, when she couldn't take it anymore, she put on her sneakers and left. Without any destination in mind, she wandered downtown, reliving the attack in the park and trying to figure out why it had happened, what it all meant, and what she should do next.

Soon she found herself passing by places that had always meant so much to her. Rockefeller Center. Saint Patrick's Cathedral. Fifth

Avenue. They all brought back happy memories of her youth, of trips arranged by Aunt Sally and Uncle Roger on holidays or other special occasions like birthdays or graduations.

Those were good times. Yet she felt oddly melancholy. Part of it, no doubt, had to do with her terrible ordeal in the park. But they'd arrested Ned Lacey, and wasn't that good news?

No, there was something else gnawing at her, something she'd missed, something she was trying to explain in her own mind. She looked at her watch, then hailed a cab, a determined look in her eyes.

Billy finally decided to call Detective Rios.

"What do you mean you can't reach her?" snapped Rios.

"We tried calling her at home several times," Billy explained. "We tried calling her at work. Her friend Anita said she never showed up. We even took a ride up to where she lives and tried to get into her apartment. When no one answered, we asked the manager to open the door.

He did, but no one was home."

"Have you any idea where she might be?" said Rios.

"We've been thinking and thinking. I'm not sure, but I have an idea. It's just a hunch."

"Where are you?"

"Outside her apartment building," said Billy.

"Stay there. We'll see you in fifteen minutes."

33

WHAT A DIFFERENCE A FEW HOURS MADE!
Thick, gray clouds had rolled in, threatening to burst and deluge
the city, when Laura's taxi stopped at the Kents' house in Queens.
She didn't expect any cars in the driveway, and there weren't any.
After paying her fare, Laura walked to the backdoor and opened it
with a key her aunt and uncle had given her in case of an emergency.
Once inside, she went directly to the basement.

With the little light that managed to filter through the dirty
windows, she threaded her way through the layers of dust and
clutter to the area where Aurora's personal belongings were
boxed. After turning on the overhead light, she located the carton
that Alex had been examining that day. She flipped through the
albums first. The photos of the wedding were stunning. One, in
particular, caught her attention. Her mom and dad are coming
out of the church, smiles of pure joy on their faces. Everyone
around them is beaming, too. Everyone, except Roger Kent, who
had married Sally only months before.

Looking through a stack of loose photographs at the bottom
of the box, Laura discovered more pictures of Aurora and Roger
laughing and embracing. On the back of one were the words
"Two years, two months to the wedding. Ours!" Learning that
her mother and Uncle Roger once had a romantic relationship

was one thing. Discovering that they had planned to get married jolted Laura and left her trembling. How was something like that kept from her for all those years? What other secrets lay waiting to be revealed?

She sifted through another box. There, she found mostly business correspondence between Lorne and the studio or his agent along with a bundle of letters from his fan club. Buried in the batch was a letter from Aurora in New York City to Lorne in Los Angeles, dated two weeks before Aurora was killed. In it, she noted that—"three times over the past week"—Roger had asked her to dinner, just the two of them, without Sally. "I was flabbergasted. Naturally, I said No each time," Aurora wrote. "I don't think that pleased R. Old flames die hard, I guess. I hope I didn't hurt his feelings."

Laura reread the letter. Why would Uncle Roger want to take his sister-in-law, a new mother, out to dinner without his wife? There seemed to be only one answer: To rekindle an old flame that he never fully extinguished.

She put the letter in her pocket and began riffling through others. Suddenly, she sensed a presence behind her. She spun around. "Did you find what you were looking for?" asked Uncle Roger, a strange, probing look in his eyes.

A flash of lightning was followed by a sharp clap of thunder.

"Oh, you startled me, Uncle Roger," said Laura.

"I wish you had told me you were coming," he remarked, surveying the open boxes. "I would have put a stronger light in here."

"Aren't you supposed to be working?" she inquired.

"Yes, but when Anita called and told me no one had heard from you or knew where you were, I got worried. I left work and came here. I just knew you'd be here."

"Why'd you think that?"

"Once Aunt Sally told me you'd been in the basement, I knew you'd be back. You have a lot of questions, and there may be answers here. Right?"

"Yes." Then with the apprehension and excitement of someone

entering unexplored territory, she said, "Why didn't you tell me you and my mother were planning to get married?"

"Oh, that! That was all before your mother met your dad ... ancient history," he replied, laughing slightly. "What was the point? What were we supposed to do, sit you down when you were twelve or thirteen and say, 'Here's something you should know: Your mother and I were once deeply in love'? We decided not to complicate your life."

She felt more emboldened. "So, what else didn't you tell me, Uncle Roger?"

"Nothing." He seemed nervous now.

Rumblings outside suggested the sky was about to break open again.

"Didn't you try to reignite the spark between you and my mother?"

"No, not really."

"Didn't you ask her out—just you and her, without Aunt Sally—only a couple of weeks before she was murdered?"

He leaned up against the paneling. Roger was out of uniform now, and his jacket was open. Laura could see his revolver in its holster. "Now you're getting too personal. I just wanted to have dinner with your mother for old times' sake."

"You're lying!" she cried out. "It was more than that."

"No ... I'm not!" he insisted. "It's true your mom was very special to me, but by the time I started going out with Aunt Sally, it was over between your mother and me."

Laura pulled the letter out of her pocket and began reading the part in which Aurora noted that—"three times over the past week"—Roger had asked her out to dinner, just the two of them, without Sally. Then this:

> *I was flabbergasted. Naturally, I said No each time. I don't think that pleased R. Old flames die hard, I guess. I hope I didn't hurt his feelings.*

"Does that sound like it was over with you?" she asked.

"You're making too much of it," said Roger, sweat beading his forehead now.

From the top of the stairs came a woman's voice. "Is that you down there, Roger?" Sally asked hesitantly.

"Yes, Sal."

"Who are you talking to? I hear voices."

"It's Laura," he replied.

Sally ventured farther down the stairway. A flashlight held loosely in her hand cast eerie shadows on the wall.

"What are you two doing down here?" asked Sally. She looked around inquisitively, a stranger to her own basement.

"Just talking, Sal," said Roger.

"Hi, Aunt Sally," Laura added in a soft, flat voice.

"What are you talking about?" Sally inquired, peering into the room with Aurora's belongings.

Neither Roger nor Laura answered at first. Then Laura spoke up. "I came here to see if I could find some more information about my parents. I was looking through the photos and letters and ..."

Roger broke in. "Let's all go upstairs. It's too hot and dark down here."

Sally ignored him. "And what did you find, darling?"

"I was looking for clues that might tell me who murdered my mother."

"Did you find any?"

"I'm not sure. I think so."

"Let's go," Roger insisted.

"YOU GO!" Sally shouted, her face on fire in the dim light. "What did you discover?" she continued, her voice softer again.

Laura paused for what seemed like an eternity. "I learned that Uncle Roger and my mother once had a romantic relationship. I learned that they had planned to get married." Then, drawing a deep breath, she added, "I learned that just two weeks before my mother was murdered ..."

Roger grabbed his wife under the arm and pulled her toward the stairway. Sally yanked away from him. "Damn it, leave us alone, Roger." Then, turning to Laura, she said, "I know what Uncle Roger did. He's still paying for it. So am I."

"I'm not paying for anything because I did nothing wrong," he declared, seemingly offended.

"YOU DID NOTHING WRONG?" Laura exploded. "You murdered my mother, didn't you?"

"No, No," he replied.

"You had a motive. Weren't you angry, dejected, and crazy when my mother rejected you?" she pressed on.

"No, it wasn't like that at all."

"What was it like, then?"

"I wouldn't do anything to harm her. I loved her too much," he confessed. "I still do."

"YOU SILLY, OLD FOOL!" Sally bellowed. "You're still clinging to the hope she'll come back to you, even now that she's dead. Sometimes, I think it should have been you, and not Aurora."

Laura could not believe what she was hearing, and the change in her aunt's behavior was extraordinary. It brought back memories of moments when Aunt Sally flew into a rage over something as simple as the time she overcooked the Thanksgiving turkey. Yes, YES. Laura was certain that those rare times, when Aunt Sally lost control of her emotions, were the something she had been missing, what she had forgotten. She looked at her aunt with new interest.

Sally flopped into a chair, anguish and defeat in her face where there was a sense of peace, the sureness of faith, and the glare of hope. "I loved Aurora," she volunteered. "She was my only sister. We were so close, ever since we were kids. But we had our differences, and I hated her for some of the things she did, and what she was. Aurora was this, Aurora was that! Aurora was the beautiful one! Aurora was the smart one! Aurora was the outgoing one! Aurora married the movie star! Aurora had the child we couldn't have! God knows, we tried."

It was as if her face crumpled for a moment.

"Thank God, you came along, darling," Aunt Sally added, back in control.

Thunder rolled in the distance

"I can sympathize with the hurt you felt, Aunt Sally," said Laura, her eyes glistening. "I'm sorry you couldn't have children of your own. But did you ever feel so angry with her, and jealous, that ... "

"Let's go upstairs, Sal!" snapped Roger.

"Just shut up, Roger!"

Laura finished her thought, "Did you kill your sister, Aunt Sally?"

A palpable silence fell, and the heat was suffocating.

"There's a time for everything. Maybe this is the time to talk," said Sally, taking a deep breath that seemed to pain her. "I couldn't help myself," she began. "When I found out that Roger wanted to see Aurora again, it was the last straw. I realized he never stopped loving her. I went crazy. Now she was going to take my husband away from me!"

Roger jumped in, directing his comments to Laura. "When that rotten bitch in the station house called my Sal to spread that dirty lie, I tried to calm her down," he explained. "There was nothing to it. Just two old friends getting together for dinner. But Sally wouldn't listen. Even when your father came back to New York, she never really got over it."

Sally dismissed him with a wave of her hand.

"So, what happened next?" asked Laura.

"One night, when Uncle Roger was at work and your dad was out with his pals," said Sally, "I drove into the city. I had no trouble getting into your parents' building and into their apartment. Outside of your mom and dad, we were the only ones who had keys to the place, and I was a frequent visitor, especially after you were born."

She took another deep breath, then continued. "When I let myself into the apartment, your mother was sleeping on the sofa and you were asleep in your room. With all of this rage building and building in me, I went straight into your parents' bedroom where I knew your father kept his gun, took the gun out of the side table, and put it in my purse."

She paused. "By the time I returned to the living room, your mother was awake. She seemed startled to see me. I didn't give her a chance to say anything. I took out the gun and shot her. I heard her cry out, 'Oh, no, oh, Sally,' and then she fell to the floor. I ran out of the house. On the way home, I threw the gun into the river."

Sally buried her face in her hands and wept.

Having been at the scene of the crime, Laura could visualize what had happened. She desperately tried to stay calm. There was so much more to learn. Finally, she turned to Uncle Roger. "Did she tell you what she did when you came home?" she asked.

"All she kept saying that night was 'God will forgive me! God will forgive me!' She didn't talk about it then, or after, but I knew something bad had happened."

"And you didn't do anything after you realized that your wife had shot Aurora?"

"I couldn't, I wouldn't."

"But you're a cop, Uncle Roger."

"It was a terrible time. I didn't know what to do," he said. "Some days, I wanted to come forward, but I was afraid. The media frenzy was incredible! Every day, someone had a new twist, a new revelation, on what happened that night, and the suspicions and outcries against your father just kept getting louder and louder. Even the police came under attack for not moving on him fast enough. And then your father disappeared ... I thought Sally would come forward then, but she didn't, and I was glad. She would have set off a new storm of news stories, and they would have crucified me at the station house. Anyway, as time went by, calls for your father's arrest stopped, or lessened, and Aunt Sally went back to her normal routine, and so did I, except we had a baby to take care of now."

"So, you did nothing!" Laura declared.

"I did nothing because Aunt Sally did nothing."

"You know what I think?" said Laura. "I think you were intimidated by Aunt Sally. You still are."

"I did what I thought was best."

"You sure did. You allowed Aunt Sally to raise the child of the woman she murdered and the one you say you loved," said Laura.

"What should I have done?" he asked. "Aunt Sally is a good

woman, basically. What she did was in a fit of jealous rage, a moment of uncontrollable anger. And look how well she took care of you."

"And so, you let my father take the blame all these years for her and for you." Haven't heard enough, Laura headed for the stairs, then stopped. "And why didn't you tell me about the money my dad sent you and Aunt Sally over the years to take care of me?" she asked.

He seemed surprised she knew about that. "It's what your father wanted," he explained. "He preferred to be anonymous when it came to your financial support." He walked toward her. "Where're you going? I thought we could ..."

Heavy footsteps could be heard overhead now. They were moving in different directions, as if someone were running from room to room. It may have been that he panicked or he did what a cop instinctively would do. Uncle Roger pulled out his gun.

As he did, bolts of lightning followed by tremendous claps of thunder shook the house, shutting off the lights. Footsteps came pounding down the stairs and across the basement floor. A gunshot was heard, then another, followed by crashing bodies, objects exploding into pieces, and piercing screams, groans and vulgarities, all under a cloud of gunpowder smoke and the musty smell of neglect.

"Got him, got him!" someone screamed. When the lights came on again, Detective Rios and a uniformed policeman were pinning Uncle Roger to the ground. Detective Levine had her arms around Aunt Sally. Billy found Laura behind some boxes, her arms folded over her head and her legs tucked under her, like a turtle in the defensive posture. He bent over and gently turned her around. "Thank God you're alive," he cried, helping her to her feet.

After Laura briefed Rios about the confessions, Uncle Roger was cuffed and led upstairs. He kept shouting, "I'M A GOOD COP! I'M A GOOD COP!" Aunt Sally went quietly. "Pray for me," she pleaded when she was ushered out of the house and into a police car.

34

By the time Laura emerged from the house with Billy, the rain had stopped and the sky was clearing. Alex and Anita ran over to them and hugged them. No one said anything; they didn't have to. They were all alive.

Detective Rios came out the backdoor. When she spotted him, Laura ran up the driveway and embraced him. Not sure how to react, Rios patted her gently on the back and asked her how she was doing. "Good," she replied, "all things considered."

She told him she was relieved to know that her father didn't murder her mother, but at the same time she was sad for her aunt and uncle, who, after all, had acted as parents for most of her life. Rios sighed. "Look, Ms. Bennett," he said, "what your aunt did was a terrible thing, and you were only a few feet away when it happened. Your uncle only made matters worse for everyone, especially your father, for covering up for his wife. Justice is justice."

Laura understood. In whispered tones, she asked Rios whether there was anything new on the Lacey brothers. Rios led her over to the patio area, and they both sat down. Confidentially, he told her that both men were in custody now.

"Between you and me," he said, "those two guys don't like each other. Basically, one ratted out the other. Ned swore he was not on the roof that night. He swore it was Reggie, not him. Makes sense. You know how much they look alike. And besides, Ned's alibi held up."

"Of course, it usually does," said Laura.

"Now when Reggie was told what Ned said, at first he denied he was on the roof, but later admitted he *was* there, but only to have a smoke. During the next two hours, after a lot of back and forth—and I guess he felt backed into a corner—Reggie pleaded for mercy and tried to cop a plea. In the end, he admitted he might have shoved Richie 'a little,' but Ned made him do it. He said the $15,000 he had on him when the police picked him up was what Ned gave him for doing it. And that makes sense, too."

"Unbelievable," said Laura. "But there's still something I don't understand. If Ned Lacey didn't murder my mom, why did he want Richie Frisco and me dead?"

"We're working on that one," Rios replied.

Anita was still at the scene after Laura returned to Manhattan with Billy and Alex. She was fascinated by it all, even though most of the action in and around the Kent house had subsided. Most of the neighbors who had been watching the comings and goings from across the street dispersed and returned home and turned on their TVs to find out what had happened.

Anita knew, but she remained on watch. She was particularly interested in Rios' actions. Every time he came out of the house he dialed someone on his cell phone and when he didn't get any answer slapped down the cover. Finally, she walked across the street and said, "Would you like to try mine? It works like a charm, usually."

"Oh, no thanks," he replied. "It's not the phone."

"Sorry. That happens to me a lot," said Anita. She paused. "Oh, I'm Anita Tedesco."

"I know who you are. I know all of Laura's friends."

"And I know who you are. I know all of Laura's detectives."

He laughed.

"Now that's better," she said. "You've been walking around with this serious mask on all afternoon."

"It comes with the job."

"I have a job, but I try not to take it too seriously."

"What do you do?"

"I'm a media planner in an advertising agency."

"Nice, but that's not life or death, Ms. Tedesco," he suggested.

"Wanna bet?"

The handsome man smiled an infectious smile.

"You look like you could use a break, Detective. What do you say we get some coffee?"

"Sure, why not? Call me Carlos."

"And you can call me Anita."

35

LAURA WAS UP EARLY THE FOLLOWING MORNING when Detective Rios called and asked her to come downtown. He didn't explain why he wanted to see her except to say that it was important.

Rios was waiting in his office when she arrived. "I'd be obliged if you kept this confidential," he said as he led her down an aisle through a bustling room of detectives and their associates. "Since you put so much time and effort in this case I thought you should meet someone who wants to meet you."

When they entered a private office, she was introduced to Frances Lacey, Ned's wife. Laura was flabbergasted. In the awkwardness of the moment, she didn't know whether to shake her hand or turn around and leave. They shook hands.

"I'm so sorry for the pain and suffering you've had to go through," said Frances, "and I'm sorry for whatever I did or didn't do to cause you so much pain." Laura didn't know what to say. Who really knew how much she went through over the years?

Rios motioned everyone to sit down. "After Mrs. Lacey gave us a statement earlier this morning," he explained, "she wanted to talk with you personally and tell you the facts as she knows them. That's why I asked you to come down here."

"That's fine," said Laura, "but why didn't she say something earlier?"

"I don't really know," Frances replied. "You've got to remember it was my husband who was involved."

"I don't get it," Laura pointed out. "If your husband didn't kill my mother, how was he involved?"

"Let me try to explain," Frances continued. "I'm not saying my husband is, or ever was, an angel, but this all happened twenty-two years ago. We were young, we'd just had a child, and Ned had borrowed a lot of money from loan sharks to start up his own business. When he couldn't pay off the loans, he tried to find a way to get the money. He was a desperate man. Then along came your father out of Chaney's Bar that night, and Ned got this idea. He'd invite Lorney up to our apartment, give him a few drinks on top of what he already had, chain him to a steam pipe, and hold him for ransom 'just for a couple of days,' until he got enough money to pay off his debts. And that's what he tried to do."

"Desperate? He must have been crazy," said Laura.

"Maybe, but desperate people do crazy things sometimes," said Frances.

"And short-term kidnappings were not an unusual way for some hustlers to raise money back then in the neighborhood," Rios added.

"As you may or may not know," Frances continued, "I was very fond of your father. In fact, we were very close at one time, before he met your mother. Anyway, I didn't want any part of my husband's scheme, and I told him so. Then it started getting ugly. Your father kept demanding that Ned unchain him and let him go, but Ned told him to shut up. Your father was so persistent. Ned couldn't take it anymore. He pulled out a gun and threatened to shoot your dad. Your father just kept calling him names and demanding to be set free. Ned couldn't handle it anymore and slammed his gun on your father's head a couple of times, knocking him out cold."

Frances started sobbing. After gaining control, she picked up the story. "During the night, I nursed your father's wounds. There were nasty gashes on the side of his head. I gave him something to eat. We talked, and we talked. It was the first time I saw your father cry. Not because of what Ned did to him. Believe it or not, he talked about you. He was terribly frightened of being a father. He kept saying that she, meaning you, needs someone who really knows how to take care of her."

Frances continued. "I kept arguing with Ned, but he wouldn't let Lorney go. The next afternoon, when Ned stepped out to buy some more liquor, I saw my chance. I scrambled all over the house looking for a spare key and found one in the junk drawer. I opened the lock on the chain and freed Lorney. Naturally, Ned wanted to kill me, and the baby, when he came back and found his hostage gone. He started ranting and raving. I promised I wouldn't say anything, and he finally calmed down. He always had a short fuse."

Rios concluded, "So, mum was the word for years, or until the story began leaking out and people started poking around."

Laura finished the thought. "And Richie Frisco paid the ultimate price for poking around. I suppose I would have been next."

Rios nodded.

"I suppose Ned was scared he'd be charged and convicted of kidnapping," Laura concluded.

"Exactly," Rios agreed.

"You don't know Ned," sobbed Frances. "He's not a terrible man. He's just terrified of so many things, but especially of being locked away. He'd do anything to stay out of prison."

Laura was unconvinced he didn't have any other choices.

"I couldn't stand it anymore," Frances continued. "Enough was enough. All those years. The lying, the shame, the terror. Afraid the police would come in the middle of the night and drag us out of bed. And now the senseless killing of a good man like Richie Frisco. I had to come forward, regardless of the consequences."

There was nothing more to say. Laura looked at her watch and got up. "I'm sorry, but I really have to leave."

Rios accompanied her to the door. "Did she answer your questions?"

"Some," Laura replied. "I think I'm beginning to understand why my father ran away."

"Me, too," said Rios. "The pressures on him must have been enormous. His wife, his soul mate, is suddenly murdered. With all the sorrow and pain and anger he's feeling, he's making arrangements for her funeral. Then the awful rumors start, and they keep hammering away, linking your father to the murder. As if he didn't have enough to worry him, he's concerned about Frances Lacey. The last thing he wants to do is put her in harm's way with that madman. After all, Frances was your father's first serious love."

"And don't forget the baby in the crib," Laura added.

"Oh, yes. Very important. With everything else going on, he doesn't feel he's ready to be a father, especially after your mother dies. In fact, I think he's terrified of fatherhood. If he only knew how great you turned out ..."

She smiled.

36

TWICE IN THE PAST FEW DAYS, LAURA HAD faced death, and twice she had cheated it, and in the process so many secrets were revealed. But neither Laura nor Billy nor Alex discussed any of those matters as they sat in Laura's favorite Chinese restaurant later that day. It would be a farewell dinner. The talk was about returning home—Billy and Alex were heading back to Arizona the next morning—and getting Alex ready for school.

"What grade are you in?" asked Laura.

"Seventh," she said glumly.

"You don't seem too happy about that," said Laura.

"Believe it or not, she loves school," Billy noted. "She's very good at it."

"I believe it," said Laura, hoping Alex might have something to add.

"I don't want to go home," she finally said, her head in the palm of her hand. "I love it here. I love everything about the city. This is where the action is."

"That's for sure. Maybe too much action sometimes," Laura laughed.

"I want to be a part of the city," Alex went on. "There's so much to do here, so much to be done."

Laura reflected for a moment, then said, "Because you're

leaving doesn't mean you can never return. You go and finish school, then come back, if you like. New York needs people like you."

Alex looked up, her eyes glistening. "I'm going to miss you, Laura. I miss you already."

Laura put her arm around the girl's shoulder. "And I miss you already, Alex."

At that moment, the woman who owned the restaurant came over to the table, a concerned look on her face. "Little girl not like food?"

"Oh, no, it's fine," said Billy.

"Yes, it's very good," Alex agreed.

"Good." Then, turning to Laura, the woman said, "Mr. Scotty back now?"

Laura decided not to continue the charade. "Mr. Scotty is not coming back."

"Oh, sorry," said the woman. She turned to Billy and observed with a bluntness no one expected, "Good-looking man. Nice catch for someone."

"Sure is," Laura agreed with a grin.

As they continued eating, Laura was asked about her plans for the future. "Stay out of trouble," she replied. "Maybe, if they still love me at work, I'll take a few days off for a little R and R."

"I hope we'll see you in Arizona," said Billy.

"Oh, I'll be there," she declared. "Can't get enough of those sunsets."

Billy reached across the table and held her hand.

"Oh, don't tell me you guys are an item," Alex teased.

"Why not?" Laura laughed.

When they finished, the three of them walked to Laura's apartment building. Leaning over and hugging Alex, Laura said. "Have fun in school."

"Call me. You have my cell," Alex reminded her.

"I will."

Laura and Billy stood looking at each other for what seemed like an eternity. The glow and longing in their eyes said they desperately wanted each other and would see each other again.

"Goodbye," said Billy.

"So long," said Laura. They kissed.

There was no point prolonging it. They were all exhausted. Alex reached into her purse and offered Laura a throat lozenge. "One for the road," she insisted. Laura took it. Smiling and waving, Laura opened the door and walked into the lobby. What would she have done without her friends from Arizona?

As Laura headed for the elevator, she spotted Charlie, the doorman, who was just coming on duty. She walked over to him and said, "Excuse me, Charlie. I was just wondering. When I was coming home the other day, you were outside, talking with this man, a tall man in a cowboy hat. Someone you know?"

"No, not really," said Charlie. "Just a nice guy in a cowboy hat. He bought me some coffee, talked about the city, asked me about the building, the apartments, the people who live here. He looked like a tourist, but didn't sound like one. Just a nice guy with a healthy curiosity."

"Thanks, Charlie."

"You're welcome. Did he look like anyone you know?"

"I'm not sure."

"Well, have a good night, Ms. Bennett."

"You too, Charlie," she said, glancing over her shoulder at the man just entering the lobby. He was tall and handsome. He had on light blue jeans, a tan blazer, and a worn cowboy hat.

Something about the way he carried himself. The strength in his face, the intensity of his pale blue eyes, and the sadness around his mouth, all reminded Laura of someone. Several images flashed through her mind: The stranger unpacking his things from a van ... someone she bumped into as she was going to work one morning ... the man at the curb, his face only partially visible, who was talking to Charlie. When she noticed that the man in the lobby had a fresh bruise on his cheek, her heart skipped a couple of beats.

As she began walking toward him, the man removed his cowboy hat and smiled warmly. In an instant, she remembered another image, one from the many photos she saw in the basement. It showed a good-looking young man smiling warmly as he stood on a street in New York City. Was the man in the photo and the man in the lobby one and the same, separated by years of life experiences?

She drew closer, fearing the worst: What if he was not the person she thought he was? She felt like running to him and discovering, once and for all, who he was, but she dared not. Finally, she and the man stood face to face, eye to eye. Hopelessly unable to hide her apprehension and excitement, she said, "Are you my father?"

It seemed like the man's face was transformed before her eyes. Where there was an aura of sadness and loneliness, there was now a blend of hope and joy, and a little trepidation.

"Yes, Laura, I am," he whispered.

Laura gently touched his cheek. "Thanks for saving my life," she said.

He reached out and held her hand. "I heard the news about what happened in Queens. Thanks for believing in me."

They hugged. "We have a lot to talk about," said Laura, leading him to the elevator.

"We sure do."

As they walked, hand in hand, across the lobby, Charlie came over to them. "So, you know each other, after all," he said, a big grin on his face.

"It's a long story, Charlie, but meet my father," said Laura with pride.

The End